TOXIC

VOWS

~~~~~~~~~~~~~~~~~~

The Seacastle Mysteries

Book 4

PJ Skinner

ISBN 978-1-913224-47-9

Parkin Press
INDEPENDENT PUBLISHER

Cover design by Mariah Sinclair

Discover other titles by PJ Skinner

The Seacastle Mysteries

Deadly Return (Book 1)

Eternal Forest (Book 2)

Fatal Tribute (Book 3)

Mortal Vintage (Book 5 pending)

Mortal Mission: A Murder mystery on Mars

Written as Pip Skinner

The Green Family Saga (written as Kate Foley)

Rebel Green (Book 1)

Africa Green (Book 2)

Fighting Green (Book 3)

The Sam Harris Adventure Series

Fool's Gold (Book 1)

Hitler's Finger (Book 2)

The Star of Simbako (Book 3)

The Pink Elephants (Book 4)

The Bonita Protocol (Book 5)

Digging Deeper (Book 6)

Concrete Jungle (Book 7)

Also available as box sets on Amazon and AI narrated audiobooks on other retailers

Go to the PJ Skinner website for more info and to purchase paperbacks directly from the author: https://www.pjskinner.com

Dedicated to my brother Charlie

Harriet

Best Wishes

from

Chapter 1

November had arrived with a vengeance in Seacastle. The seagulls were huddled on the beach like grey pensioners carping about the cold. Muddy waves threw themselves against the pebbles, rubbing off their sharp edges and making them roll down into the surf. The windfarm had drawn a bank of cloud around itself and lurked out on the horizon invisible from shore. A keen north-easterly breeze cut down the side streets at right angles to the promenade and blew itself out over the channel. The Grotty Hovel faced west onto the street, but the warped back door let in a freezing draught which I couldn't stem. I couldn't afford to heat my little house during the day, never mind replace the back door, so I had taken to wearing so many clothes I walked like the Michelin Man. The income generated by my vintage furniture shop, Second Home, had not yet received it's Christmas bump, as people stayed indoors in the foul weather. Trade became deader than skinny jeans.

A thump on the ceiling told me Mouse's mood rivalled mine. He had shut himself into his room and refused to come out (except for meals) since his father, my ex-husband, D.I. George Carter, had informed him that he would be getting a sibling. Mouse and George did not have a great relationship at the best of times, but Mouse had been an only child for his whole life, and the new arrival would intrude on their dynamic. I had prior knowledge of the impending birth, and I happened to know that George was not as pleased as he might have been with this development, but I couldn't dredge up any sympathy for him. When Mouse stomped into the house muttering about betrayal, I had tried to reason with him, but sometimes the challenge of communicating with a sensitive teenager remained outside my comfort zone.

Mouse, (real name Andrew Carter) had moved in with me for a short stay after my divorce from George, and never left. I took him in to annoy George as much as anything, but Mouse had become part of my life, and wormed his way into my heart in a way I would have found extraordinary less than a year ago. An intelligent boy, with a talent for hacking, Mouse had suffered from neglect and had been sidelined a lot since his mother died. Now his father had announced that Sharon Walsh, my replacement, was pregnant, and he intended to marry her in short order. I couldn't blame Mouse for feeling unloved. George had a talent for crushing people's hopes.

Hades, our rescue cat, yowled at me from his basket, claiming extreme hunger and bad treatment. He ate only the most expensive cat food available, using up more than his fair share of the food budget, with me feeling even more grumpy as a consequence. I made myself a cup of coffee and scrolled mindlessly on my phone, enjoying watching cat videos of adorable kittens who were sweet natured and funny, and being unfaithful to Hades. I cast a resentful glance at the Lloyd Loom laundry basket where he liked to hide from my pathetic attempts at taming him. He loved everyone else, it's just me he couldn't stand. I think he did it to annoy me.

My mobile phone started to vibrate and skipped across the table watched by a fascinated Hades, who emerged from the laundry basket attracted by the buzzing. Before he could swipe at it and send it crashing to the floor, I picked it up and looked at the screen. George. What now? I sighed and put it to my ear.

'Tan, it's me.'

'What do you want? It had better not be wedding related. I'm not in the mood. You son is having a three-day tantrum upstairs, and I'm at the end of my tether.'

'Don't be mean. You're getting rid of me at last. I'd have thought you'd be thrilled to push me down the aisle.'

He had a point. His inability to make up his mind where Sharon and I were concerned had long been a bone of contention. Only the pregnancy had stopped him trying persuade me to take him back, despite me assuring him that hell would freeze over first. I took a deep breath.

'I'd rather push you over a cliff to be honest, but I'm listening.'

'Good girl. I knew you'd come round. After all, this baby will be your step-child.'

'No, it won't. I've already inherited one of your children. I won't be taking the next one. He or she will be one hundred percent your problem.'

A scuffling noise behind me made me turn around, but I could only see Hades on the stairs.

'That's not why I called,' he said. 'I need your help.'

'What sort of help?'

'Sharon wants me to organise the wedding.'

I couldn't prevent the spontaneous guffaw from escaping my throat.

'You? A wedding?'

'Exactly. That's why I'm calling you. Can you do it for me?'

The cheek of the man! I couldn't think of an answer that didn't contain a string of curses. Finally, I said, 'are you mad?'

'Look, I know it's a bit weird, but we're friends, aren't we? And my son lives with you. He'll help. And can't Ghita make the cake? I'll pay for it all.'

Despite my discombobulation, I could see advantages to this plan. If Mouse helped with the wedding, he might get to know Sharon, and later, his sibling. I tried the grown-up approach.

'Can Rohan and Kieron do the catering?'

'I don't know who they are, but you decide. Can you fix the flowers too? Sharon's too busy with her business.'

'Will you pay me?'

'Pay you? What for?'

'I'm putting the phone down now.'

'Okay, but you should be glad to get rid of me.'

'Oh, I am, but not glad enough to do it for free. I'll send you an offer.'

'I've got to go.'

I had a thought.

'Wait. What about her family? Have you thought of how they'll take this bit of news?'

'It's none of their business. They're not paying. That sister of hers is quite happy to sit back and enjoy the benefits of Sharon marrying a D.I.'

I had not found being married to a D.I. had enhanced my life much, but I let it slide.

'I'd be more worried about her dodgy brother-in-law. Hasn't he got a record?'

'Not for violence. He won't object. I can't see Fintan Hurley arranging the flowers for the church.'

'Hasn't he objected to Sharon marrying into the force?'

'I don't see it's any of his business. He's not marrying me.'

I sighed.

'Okay. But if I have any trouble with him, I'll let you organise the wedding yourself. When is it?'

'The twenty-first.'

'Of November? You're having a laugh.'

'Don't be so dramatic. It's not difficult to organise a large party. You used to do this all the time. Oh, the Super's here. Bye.'

Typical. But why had I said yes? What had possessed me? I let my heart rule my head as usual. Talk about short notice. But then I realised Joy and Ryan from the Shanty pub could provide the drinks. Roz could arrange the flowers and waitress at the wedding, Ghita could make the cake, and Rohan and Kieron could cater. Times were tough for all of us in the early winter lull. And it might be fun to work together.

I reached for a notebook and a pen and sat at the table. I chewed the end of the pen as I mulled over the offer. What would Sharon think? Surely, she would be the biggest obstacle? Wouldn't she have a fit when she discovered who would arrange her wedding? We used to get on when she worked at the reception in the police station, before she seduced George, and to be honest, she had done me a favour releasing me into the wild. Maybe we could come to some agreement. I didn't hold the affair against her, so maybe she didn't care either. Footsteps on the stairs made me turn around. Mouse froze halfway down with a large rucksack on his back. I stared at him for a moment, taking in his solemn face and the bag.

'You going somewhere?' I asked.

'And what do you care?'

I blinked and stood up.

'What brought this on? I thought we were going for a takeaway with Harry tonight.'

'I heard you,' he said, sinking down to sit on a step, balancing his rucksack on the step above. 'I'm not staying here anymore.'

'You heard me? What did I say?'

But I knew. Oh blast. I couldn't believe I had been so careless.

'About inheriting me. I thought you liked having me here. I'm leaving.'

I walked towards him and he looked away, his muscles working in his cheeks.

'Sweetheart. You can't go. I need you to feed Hades and fix my computer.'

I meant it as a joke, but the look he gave me told me I had made a mistake.

'I'm George's son. You've got stuck with me. I can see that. No wonder Harry won't move in. Well, now's your chance.'

He tried to stand up, but the weight of the rucksack dragged him back down. He started pulling at the straps and making frustrated noises. I moved close to the stairs.

'For heaven's sake. Why can't you trust me? I love you more than a son. George is an idiot and I shouldn't have said what I did, but I said it to annoy him, not to hurt you. It's not true, not at all.'

'I'm being replaced,' he said, his voice catching in his throat. 'George is having a new baby and you don't want me.'

'Don't tell me what I want. You can't leave. I won't let you.'

I stood at the bottom of the stairs and grabbed a spindle either side of the steps. I must have looked ridiculous, but I didn't know what else to do.

'Seriously?' he said. 'You're going to block the stairs? How long before you need to go to the toilet?'

'I can last at least five minutes. I may have to pee my pants.'

A tiny smile crept across his lips. He looked at me through his giraffe lashes.

'I'm sorry for overreacting. I'm feeling vulnerable and teenage with the usurper on the way.'

Letting go of the spindles, I walked up a couple of stairs and pushed him to one side, squeezing in beside him on the staircase.

'You are allowed to be vulnerable and teenage. I'm an idiot. I was trying to hurt George, not you. You're not going anywhere. Harry would dump me if I lost you. And Hades. You're my insurance.'

'Insurance?'

'My guarantee of love, given and taken. You're the glue in the Grotty Hovel. It would fall down without you.'

'Really?'

'Really. Don't milk me for compliments. Anyway, I need your help.'

'What with?'

'Your father wants us to plan his wedding.'

He turned to stare at me, his eyes wide.

'But you said no, right?'

'I'm afraid not. I felt sorry for him. And I want him to be happy without me.'

'No wonder you need me. You're not very bright.'

'Sharon can't be the sharpest tool in the box either.'

'There's no accounting for taste.'

Chapter 2

Shellshock struck me quite soon after my ill-advised agreement to organise George's wedding. I had very little idea how to pull it off, but, luckily, the time span available for planning was so short that I didn't have time to brood. The Christmas rush, such as it was, would be upon me almost immediately afterwards. This meant I had to get the shop decorated and my small stock in prominent places, but out of reach of shoplifters, as soon as possible. I also had to unpack and clean anything likely to sell as a present from the boxes of stock at the back of the shop.

Before starting in earnest, I had to complete a house clearance with my partner in crime, Harry Fletcher, ex-army, with a shaved head and a barrel chest, and the softest heart this side of the planet. We were also an item, although we had navigated stormy seas since getting together this year. In some respects, we had remarkably similar trajectories. He was trying to reconcile with his brother, while I had recently done so with my older sister, Helen. Both Harry and I had been married, but neither of us had children, and I could not be sure we were done with that yet. I could still technically have a baby, although I would qualify as an unkindly-named geriatric mother, and would need to get a wiggle on if I still wanted to try. We had skirted around the topic, but mostly we got by with Mouse and Hades, our surrogate offspring. Sometimes you have to deal with your baggage before setting sail on a new adventure.

I put some bacon in the air-fryer, an early Christmas present from Helen, who has made it her business to improve my life in every way since her unexpected separation from her husband, Martin. This event shocked me almost as much as it did her. I never imagined them breaking up, but then she had not always been entirely honest with me when it came to her life. She had always concentrated on my short comings, and blamed me for my break up with George, to deflect from the fact her perfect marriage had been a sham.

For once, after the revelation of Sharon's pregnancy, she had been kinder, realising, perhaps, that all was in fact lost, and George had no intention of coming back to me. I did not tell her about his reluctance to marry Sharon, or his attempts to reconcile with me. I felt we had enough complications in our lives without further muddying the waters. Helen's decision to move to Seacastle permanently had surprised and alarmed me in equal measure, but we were both making an effort to get on better, and seeing her so distraught had made it easier for me to remember how much I loved her despite everything.

I rescued the bacon and made a couple of breakfast butties for Harry and me, dropping a piece beside the laundry basket for ratbag, to prevent a fit of sulking. Since Mouse had not made an appearance yet, I put extra bacon in our butties and wrapped them in waxed paper. The amazing smell made my mouth water. Does anything smell as good as crispy bacon? I made a flask of sweet coffee for Harry and placed both the flask and the butties in a satchel. A horn sounded outside and I realised I had committed the cardinal sin of being late for our rendezvous. Harry's punctuality rivalled that of a clock, whereas I tended to be more casual, or even fashionably late. My habits had improved since I started working with him, and I discovered quite soon that a hot bacon butty could dispel any doubts over my time keeping.

I grabbed my long, down coat from the peg beside the door and pulled a cashmere beanie over my head. The matching scarf dangled from the pocket of the coat, and I fished it out and wrapped it around my neck a couple of times. They were early Christmas presents from Harry and felt even warmer because of the love they came with. I patted my coat pocket to check for my keys and let myself out of the front door of the terraced house and onto the street lined with similar two-up-two-down dwellings. My sister had rented a similar house in a terrace a couple of streets west of mine. She lived there with her daughter Olivia, who had left for university in Edinburgh, or as Mouse put it, 'as far away from Helen as possible'. Harsh, but it had a whiff of truth about it.

Outside in the street, Harry's van perched with two wheels on the pavement and two off. The vapour from the exhaust hung in the air and when I breathed out, the resulting trail of freezing breath meant I could pretend I still smoked. The cravings had not entirely gone, but I felt real terror at the idea of a sneaky cigarette starting me off again after all I'd done to stop. Harry waved at me. I could see the impatience etched on his face, but I waved back, pretending to be unfazed it. I grinned and pointed at my satchel. The muscles in his face relaxed as the lure of the butties did its trick.

'Hello, partner,' he said, as I got into the van. 'How about a kiss to warm the cockles of my heart?'

I had not put on any lipstick due to my anticipation of our breakfast, so I accepted his invitation with gusto. He giggled like a schoolboy which made me love him more.

'How about a bacon butty for the driver?' I said. 'Do you want to sit in the wind shelter by the sea, or is it too cold?'

'You just want to feed that darn seagull, don't you?' I smirked.

'Herbert might be hungry. It's midwinter, you know. He can't steal ice creams from the tourists at this time of year.'

'Well, I'm not freezing my butt off in the shelter. I'll eat my breakfast in the lay-by when we get out of town.' I sighed.

'Okay then, but I'll have to go by later and take him the crusts.'

Harry rolled his eyes in mock annoyance. He was not the only person who took a dim view of my habit of adopting everyone. George had complained at length when I took Mouse in, and had not been happy when I admitted that Hades the cat had also become a permanent fixture. I had buttoned my lip and not told him how little I cared about his opinions since he had abandoned me and set me up in the Grotty Hovel (now secretly my favourite place in town). In spite of our divorce, George still felt entitled to direct my life and let me know his opinions on my actions. I tolerated this annoying custom because Mouse needed his father, and I didn't take any notice anyway.

Despite the age of the bungalow which needed to be emptied, the clearance appeared to be pretty disappointing. Most of the contents were too modern for my shop, and in a terrible state of repair. We were accustomed to doing the occasional clearance when it would have been more profitable to set fire to the contents, but Harry decided to take everything to his cousin Tommy's warehouse in the east end of London anyway 'in case he could salvage a few quid'. I rescued an apothecary's chest from the bedroom, which I planned to give to Mouse for Christmas to use in his bedroom for his bits and pieces. As we were carrying a shabby, chipboard cupboard out to the van, one of the the doors fell open and an assortment of cigarette and other small decorative boxes tipped onto the ground. I put down the chest and picked a couple of them up. The boxes were filthy and needing some TLC, but I spotted a couple of gorgeous chinoiserie and lacquered boxes.

'Jackpot,' I said. 'How did we not see them in there?'

'Someone's precious collection,' said Harry, passing me a 1930s metal cigarette box with a fighter plane on the lid. 'I love this one the best.'

'Perfect for Christmas presents to sell in the shop,' I said. 'This has cheered me up no end.'

I noticed a shadow pass over his face, but he didn't say anything. I hid my glee. The metal cigarette box would not be for sale this Christmas. I grinned inwardly as I imagined his face on opening his gift.

We got back into the ancient van and Harry cranked up the heating. A slight smell of burning filled the cabin, but went away again before I plucked up courage to mention it. Harry had inherited the business from an uncle in the East End of London and the van had close to two hundred thousand miles on the clock. The dashboard still contained a cassette player which we both used to play our tapes from years ago and head bang our way along the highways of England. Harry had swapped out the old-fashioned static seat belts for modern inertia ones which made them a lot more comfortable. I suspected we were driving a vehicle which would not pass its next MOT, but I didn't comment. Harry called it an heirloom as a joke, but it had sentimental value all the same.

On the way home, I told him about the wedding and Harry roared with laughter instead of being sympathetic.

'Before Christmas?' he said. 'That's a stretch.'

'I can't believe I agreed to do it,' I said. 'George can still make me do anything he wants me too, no matter how ludicrous.'

'If I read this right, you're doing it for Mouse, not George. Mouse needs to make his peace with George before the baby arrives, because once it's here, there will be no time for reconciliations.'

'I knew you'd understand. George sold the idea to me as a way to make money too.'

'He's right, you know. You'll make some money and get rid of him in one fell swoop. Things could be worse. Take today's clearance for example.'

'What a dump. I guess they rented it out for years and didn't check on the state of the furniture. At least I got some great boxes for the shop.'

'My cousin Tommy may be able to patch up some pieces. No profit for us though.'

'The wedding may be the saving grace this month then. I wish I could find something for you to do.'

Harry grimaced.

'There is something.'

'What's that then? Can I help?'

'Look, I'll understand if you're not happy, but Grace rang me and asked me to do some deliveries.'

I am not a jealous person by nature, but Grace Wong, my upmarket competitor on Seacastle High Street, had been trying to steal Harry for months. Only for antiquing, but it made me feel insecure.

'Did she now?'

'Do you mind?'

'Of course I do, but there's no harm helping her deliver stuff. Just don't offer her a clearance or I might turn bright green and start foaming at the mouth.'

He grinned.

'Don't worry. I'll be faithful to you. Do you want to feed Herbert? I've got some stale biscuits in the glove compartment.'

Chapter 3

Both Harry and George had a point about my habit of collecting people and animals. I had practically adopted half of the town at this stage. My circle got wider, and yet closer, all the time, and the ramifications meant I was always mixed up in some drama or another. However, it also meant I could call on a large number of helpers when I needed them. I sensed that Sharon did not have anything like the village required to raise her child and I had decided we should be generous with our support. I also wanted everyone to benefit from George's largesse if possible.

I called a summit meeting at the Vintage, the café I ran over my antique shop, Second Home. With Mouse at the helm of the coffee machine, my friend, Ghita Chowdhury handed out slices of her latest delectable invention (pineapple and mint upside-down cake – yes, I know it sounds odd, but it's so good). As well as making cakes, she runs an exercise class, called Fat Fighters, which is popular due to the quantity of her products we devour. We quite often need a piece of cake to recover from Fat Fighters, so it's the perfect business model. Nobody ever accused her of being stupid. Her long dark hair hung in a thick braid down her short back and she stood on tiptoe to greet people, a habit born of her short stature.

An air of expectation hung in the air. Most people had already heard about George's upcoming nuptials, because I had already informed Roz Murray, the town foghorn, about them. She came without husband Ed, who had gone to help a friend crew his fishing boat. Roz rushed up the stairs to the café in a wafty mermaid dress of green and blue tulle, her blonde curls bouncing and her blue eyes sparkling. She whipped off her green bomber jacket and took a deep breath of the air in the Vintage, redolent with coffee and intrigue. Then she went over to the window to watch out for other arrivals, tucking her feet underneath her on the banquette.

'I still can't believe it. Our George getting married,' she said.

I shook my head at her, but I couldn't help smiling. George would have been bewildered to hear everyone call him that. He always imagined himself alone like some kind of plump lighthouse, a beacon of law in the fetid ocean of petty crime in Seacastle, but people called him Our George, like a naughty schoolboy.

'Third time lucky,' I said.

'Unlucky for some,' said Mouse. 'Sharon must be desperate.'

'Why do you all treat him like he's a teenager? He's a Detective Inspector in the Police. He can't be that childish,' said Grace Wong, picking at a piece of cake with suspicion.

'Because he behaves like a teenager,' said Joy Wells, the owner of the Shanty, in her no-nonsense style.

She had come to the summit without her husband Ryan, despite Harry offering to carry him upstairs from his wheelchair to the café. Ryan had cried off attending our summit, citing mysterious business to deal with in Prague, again. Honestly, Joy and Ryan must have thought we were all stupid. They were obviously linked to some branch of covert government operations, but we all pretended we had no idea. The Shanty pub had blossomed under their ownership, so no one complained about their odd absences or weak excuses.

'Is Max coming?' I asked Grace.

'No chance. One of our best customers is turning up this morning. We might even sell that Bentwood coat stand you left with me.'

'He's forgiven then.'

The door of the shop burst open downstairs, making the bell sway on its spring. Harry stood downstairs, hands on his thighs, panting. He waved up at the throng gathered in the café upstairs. I blew him a kiss. He beamed and wiped his bald pate with a handkerchief.

'Did I miss the cake?' he said.

'Don't worry. There's plenty left. But you're the last man in, so could you hang the closed sign on the door?'

Harry did as I instructed, and then bounded up the stairs. He put his arm around Ghita's waist.

'Where's that piece of cake then?'

'Don't manhandle the chef,' said Roz, coming to pick up her coffee. 'She'll knock your lights out.'

Ghita giggled.

'Pineapple and mint, or chocolate?'

'Not sure I'm exotic enough for the mint one, so I'll have chocolate, thank you. And a latte, please, Mouse.'

'Oh wait,' I said. 'We forgot Rohan and Kieron. Weren't they supposed to be here?'

Ghita rolled her eyes.

'They had a tiff this morning. They're not speaking to each other. Rohan went to do the shopping and Kieron is sulking in the restaurant.'

'When's Surfusion opening?' said Roz. 'Ed's keen on selling his fresh lobsters and shellfish to them.'

'Almost ready. Some teething problems with the electrics. I'm not sure January is a good month to open, to be honest. And Kieron's mother is in hospital with what he refers to as her nerves. So, it's all rather complicated.'

'Do you think they'd like to cater a wedding? They could make up some menus for the bride to choose from.'

Ghita beamed.

'If they could earn some money, it might stop them from murdering each other. Shall I ask them for you?'

Roz raised her hands to her hips and arched an eyebrow.

'It sounds suspiciously like you're organising George's wedding. Have you gone completely mad?'

Half a dozen pairs of eyes swivelled to stare at me in shock.

'Don't panic. Hear me out. We can all make money from this, well, everyone except Grace.'

'So why am I here then?' she said, arching an eyebrow.

'I knew you wouldn't like to be left out,' I said, trying not to panic. I had not thought this through. Grace and Max were nice people, but one hundred percent cash orientated. Why had I imagined she would look after the shop for me during the wedding?

Ghita jumped up and started to bounce up and down on her tiny feet.

'Can I make the cake?' she said. 'Please, please, please.'

'That is exactly what I had in mind. And can you do the flowers, Roz?'

'Do bears—'

'Honestly, Roz. Can't we go for five minutes without some lurid saying?' said Ghita.

Roz tossed her curls in defiance.

'You're such a prude. Of course, I'll take charge of the flowers. Where will we source them? They're expensive this time of year.'

'My cousin works at Covent Garden Flower market,' said Harry. 'If that's any help.'

'Do you know where they are holding it?' said Mouse.

'The flower market?' I said.

Mouse groaned.

'The wedding.'

'Oh, yes, the venue. I expect they'll use Tarton Manor House. It's got that lovely covered courtyard behind the main hotel.'

'Didn't you get married there?' said Ghita.

'George is a man of habit,' said Harry, trying not to laugh.

'It wouldn't be so bad if he hadn't married his first wife there too,' I said to general mirth.

'I think one of my cousins works in the gardens,' said Roz.

'How many cousins do you have?' I said.

'I'm not sure,' said Roz. 'My father is one of ten children.'

'No wonder you get all the juicy gossip first. Your network is extraordinary,' said Mouse. 'You're like the human worldwide web.'

Roz laughed and hugged him.

'Can we supply the drinks?' said Joy.

'Of course. That's why you're here. I really need to make a list,' I said.

'You should,' said Mouse. 'In your phone, not in a notebook. We can make a WhatsApp group for all of us to keep updated on preparations and for emergencies.'

'I don't know how to do that,' I said.

'Hand me your phone,' said Grace.

She immediately opened WhatsApp and formed a group called *George the Third*, which I found hilarious. Then she added all of our numbers to the group from my contacts. As I watched her neat fingers flash over the keyboard, I realised that the Luddite in me had not died, but threatened to revive. Mouse grinned at me.

'See,' he said. 'Grace is older than you and she knows what to do.'

Grace's finger hovered over the keyboard while she decided if this qualified as an insult or a compliment. Mouse bit his lip and looked contrite, so she went for the latter and kept typing. I took back my phone and gazed in wonder at the group.

'Excellent. Well, I guess that's it for now. I'll contact you all with specific instructions after I've spoken to Sharon.'

Roz tutted loudly.

'Haven't you forgotten the most important question of all?'

'And what's that then?'

'Does Sharon know you're organising her wedding?'

I swallowed.

'I'm not sure. Knowing George, probably not.'

'Awkward,' said Mouse, sniggering into his hand.

'Trust George to drop you in it,' said Roz.

'She may be relieved someone else is taking over,' said Ghita. 'Isn't she trying to get a new business going. I know how exhausting that is.'

'And worse when you are pregnant,' I said, without thinking.

I don't know whose jaw dropped further, but I could hear the ghost of a clank as they all hit the floor.

'Sharon's pregnant?' said Grace.

'Apparently.'

'How do you feel about it?' said Ghita, hardly daring to look me in the face.

'Crap,' I said, my voice catching in my throat, despite myself.

'That makes two of us,' said Mouse.

Harry came over and pulled us both in for a hug. I couldn't prevent a couple of rebellious tears from creeping down my face. I wiped my cheek on Harry's shoulder and kissed Mouse on the forehead.

'We'll be okay,' I said. 'And Sharon needs support right now. She's marrying a man of little self-awareness.'

'None, really,' said Joy.

'None at all,' said Grace. 'What do you want me to do for the wedding, or am I here on false pretences?'

'I hate asking, but could you cover for me here in the shop on the day of the wedding? It's a Saturday, always the day I make most money at this time of year with Christmas shoppers coming in. I promise to do the same for you whenever you need me.'

Grace smiled; the smile of a tiger meeting its prey at the watering hole. My heart tightened when I remembered she had already co-opted Harry to do deliveries for her. Would this be the coup de grace?

'I'd be happy to do that for you,' she said. 'Max can take over. And now that you mention it, I have an important antiques fair coming up after Christmas where I'll be shorthanded because Max has to go back to Hong Kong for business. Can we do a swap?'

I beamed in relief.

'It's a deal.'

Chapter 4

Sharon Walsh first entered my life when I met her at the Seacastle police station. She had been hired to staff the reception desk when Carol Burns retired. Carol's habit of swigging out of a bottle of spirits whenever she thought no one could see her had become a liability. George told me she would not accept she had a problem despite being discreetly offered a place in a rehabilitation centre. Persuading her to take redundancy had turned out to be a herculean task but the decision had been made for her. The entire station turned out to Carol's leaving do and George gave a nice speech which was out of character for him. Carol had drunk herself into a stupor and had to be helped home.

Sharon had fitted in from day one. Her no-nonsense demeanour intimidated the suspects, and no one dared talk back to her despite her relative youth. From the first day I met Sharon, I knew she would mean trouble. George stammered and blushed when he introduced us, and I realised she looked like my clone, but fifteen years my junior. After living with me in my depressed state for three years, George had come to the end of his tether. He simply didn't understand why I wouldn't just snap out of it and stop moping around, and he refused to learn about the disease. I suspect he didn't believe in depression. It seems inevitable now that he recognised Sharon as a fresh start, a chance to do it all again without the mistakes. She fawned over him, whether I was around or not. I guess she found me pathetic and not worthy of him. Either that or she thought she could spend his money faster than me.

What she hadn't realised was that I made more money than George in my job as an investigative reporter on *Uncovering the Truth*. Our nice suburban villa with two new cars parked outside relied heavily on my income to keep up the payments. When I lost my job due to depression, all our luxuries dried up as George struggled to stay afloat, but he didn't tell Sharon that. She found out when she replaced me in the beige villa. I'd have loved to have seen her face when she realised the real state of George's finances. Mind you, his mother had died recently which had brought a broad smile to his face, as not only did he resent having to visit her, but she also left him her house. I hoped George had ringfenced the money when he sold it, but he hadn't shown much financial sense while married to me.

Despite my misgivings about organising the wedding, I arranged to meet Sharon in the Ocean Café at the end of Seacastle Pier, as I didn't want her casting her beady eye over the Vintage. I'm not sure why. Maybe because she might covet that too. What Sharon wants; Sharon gets, according to George. Anyway, I loved the Ocean Café with the view from its mezzanine out over the stormy channel with swooping seagulls careering past the windows. I also thought Sharon less likely to throw a fit in a public place than in the sanctuary of my shop. I spotted her down below the mezzanine as she came through the double swing doors into the main restaurant and headed for the staircase upstairs. She mounted the stairs, looking around, as if suspecting a trap.

I pasted a large smile on my face and waved her over to the window table. She wore a powder blue suit, which looked too small for her, but I felt mean noticing it. We sat looking at each other, two clones meeting for coffee. If I had been a little older, I would have passed for her mother.

'This is a little weird,' said Sharon, brushing imaginary pieces of lint from her suit. 'I couldn't imagine what you wanted, but George let slip your arrangement.'

I froze for a second. Which arrangement? Surely not the one where I told him I wouldn't go back with him until he broke up officially with her? Even George couldn't be that indiscreet. However, she had a smirk on her face which told me she had no idea. The latest one then.

'Well, I need the money, and he needed a wedding planner so it seemed logical.'

'Logical? Weird, I'd call it, but then our George is not a sensitive soul, is he?'

I could hardly look her in the eye.

'Um, you noticed?'

She roared with laughter.

'Look, things worked out the way they did, but there's no need for us to bear a grudge, is there? I'm snowed under with work at the moment, trying to get my business off the ground. My sister and her husband need constant supervision, or they might find a way to take it over and chuck me out.'

What did she want me to say?

'Gosh. That sounds tricky.'

'I'm only half joking too. They'd be quite happy to replace me. You know how that is?'

Yes, no thanks to you, I thought, but instead I said 'it's a nightmare. And it must be harder now you are pregnant. Are you suffering from morning sickness?'

She stiffened and I wondered if George had been indiscreet again. Maybe I wasn't supposed to know? But she relaxed again.

'No, thank goodness. No symptoms yet. Except for tight trousers.'

'It doesn't show at all. How many weeks are you gone?'

'Oh, I'm not sure. We don't get much of a bump in our family. Maybe twelve weeks, so I'll still be able to fit into my wedding dress.'

'Have you bought it yet?'

'No, but I have my eye on one in the Seacastle Bridal Boutique.'

I winced. George would have to take out a second mortgage to pay for a dress from there.

'I'm sure it will be gorgeous. Are you going to have bridesmaids?'

'My sister Theresa will be maid of honour. I'm not allowed to do anything without her. She's the typical copycat younger sister. She'll probably want George when I'm finished with him.'

She gave me a smug smile. What an odd thing to say. What ever happened to 'til death do us part'?

'Since you have no objections to me being involved—'

'I didn't say that,' she said, pursing her lips.

I felt the colour rise in my cheeks, but I managed to stay calm.

'Anyway, I'd like to try and get started on the planning. The chefs at Surfusion have sent some sample menus over for you to choose from.'

I handed her the pages covered in Rohan's flowery script. She did not look at them, putting them straight into her voluminous handbag. A Birkin? I wondered who had paid for it. How come everyone had one except me? I pushed a cushion along the bench to cover up my second-hand satchel, suddenly self-conscious. I wondered why someone so young and confident would settle for George. Of course, having a baby changed the stakes. I decided to plough on and took out my notebook and pen.

'Have you chosen the flowers you want for the church?'

She raised an eyebrow.

'How Poirot of you to use a notebook. Don't you have a phone?'

'I think better in longhand. Flowers?'

'I want calla lilies in the church, and rose centrepieces for the tables.'

'Calla lilies?'

'Yes, you know, those white ones that look like vag—'

I held up a hand and nodded. Calla lilies were more common at funerals in my experience, because they signified rebirth, but seeing as she was pregnant, perhaps apt too.

'I've seen them before. I'm sure I can source some.'

I made a note and tried to remember what else I'd forgotten.

'How many people will there be at the wedding lunch?'

'Fifty so far. I'm waiting for George to finalise his list.'

'I can't imagine it will be a long one. He doesn't have many friends or relatives.'

She rolled her eyes.

'He's inviting half of Seacastle police station to make up for it. And his ex-wife.'

I tried not to laugh.

'I hear she's not so bad,' I said, gritting my teeth. 'I don't have to come you know, but Mouse won't come if I'm not invited.'

'And George wants Mouse there. I know. That's okay. If you organise the wedding, I'll be happy for you to come. Some of my relatives are not exactly my favourite people either, and they've taken a very dim view of me marrying a pig, but they're coming.'

I make a note on my pad to hide my disgust at her using that word for policeman. After all, she had worked at the station, but maybe only for money. George had often complained about Sharon, but I had taken it with a pinch of salt. I imagined it was because she had put him on a diet and stopped him eating his favourite foods and he hated that. Maybe I should have listened with more sympathy? Silly man. Too late now.

'I'll assume eighty people for now, and hurry George up for you.'

'Would you? He's being difficult.'

I felt tempted to warn her to get used to it, but what would have been the point? They were having a child together, and that made all my prejudices melt away. The poor thing needed a good start with those two as parents. I smiled again.

'Will you let me know about the menus as soon as you can? And I'll need the place settings too. Who's sitting where, and so on.'

'I hadn't thought of that. Okay, I'm on it.' She took the menus back out of her handbag. 'Let's have a look at these while we have a coffee. I think I'll have some breaded shrimp too. They're gorgeous.'

I looked at my watch.

'A bit early for me. I'll just have a latte.'

Sharon patted her stomach.

'I'm eating for two.'

I tried to smile. George had landed me right up to my neck this time. I would be well rid of him and I didn't envy her one bit. They were welcome to each other. The food arrived in double quick time. I drank my latte and tried not to watch as she wolfed down the scampi, before wiping her mouth with a napkin. She looked at her watch.

'Have you got time to come with me to Tarton Manor House on Tuesday?' she said. 'I'd like to show you the set up.'

'Sure. I'll give Rohan a call and see if he can come with use to inspect cooking facilities. Maybe the two of you can review the menus together?'

'Excellent. Is eleven o'clock okay? I'll wait there for you.'

Chapter 5

Rohan and Kieron both fancied a trip out to Tarton Manor, so I picked them up outside Surfusion. Luckily, they were excited by the opportunity to cater the wedding and were not sniping at each other like they usually did. Their relationship seemed to be based on one upmanship and hissy fits which rarely simmered down, but Ghita assured me they were happy together when I questioned her. I decided to ignore their behaviour as long as it didn't affect the wedding. If the food hit the spot, nobody would care if the chefs were at each other's throats.

'Isn't this a little weird?' said Rohan, as we drove along the wintery lanes with their stark tree lines. 'Organising your ex-husbands wedding?'

'You mean a lot weird,' said Kieron. 'Whatever possessed you?'

'I'm not sure. We still get on, and his son lives with me, so I try to keep our relationship civil. I'm trying to see it as a purely financial transaction. I get the pleasure of being paid for working with my friends, who also benefit.'

'So weird then?' said Rohan.

I grinned.

'You have no idea how unspeakably odd I find it. But George's reaction to my offer made it worth it.'

'Did you charge him a lot?'

'I'm pretty sure he fainted.'

Kieron laughed.

'You're right though. If you can bear to organise it, we'll all make money. What's the bride of Godzilla like?'

'Godzilla-like.'

They both laughed.

'She'll be no match for us,' said Kieron.

'Don't bet on it.'

Sharon waited for us in her car parked outside the stunning main house with its tall symmetrical sash windows evenly spaced above and on either side of the porticoed front door. I followed her vehicle along the driveway leading around the back of the building to the service entrance. Tarton Manor House had originally been a standalone Georgian rectory with a kitchen garden out the back, but successive owners had enlarged it by adding mismatched wings on either side of the main building. One of the wings had been constructed as a high covered courtyard with a kitchen on one side and a two-storey add-on attaching it to the main the house. The add-on had a passageway running through it to the main house off which there were toilet blocks on the ground floor and changing rooms above. Iron railings ran the length of the upper storeys interspersed with grotesque stone gargoyle flowerpots facing out over the passageway leading to the covered courtyard.

We entered the courtyard through the back door by the kitchens and were bathed in winter sunlight coming in vertical bands through the glass walls. A wave of nostalgia swept over me as I remembered my beloved parents greeting me with a hug at the top table at my wedding to George. His mother had not been so enthusiastic, but I had ignored her frosty demeanour. She had never warmed to me, but then she didn't try. George's first wife had been her favourite, having produced a son before falling victim to cancer; Andrew

Carter, my surrogate son, Mouse to his friends and I wondered what George's mother had made of Mouse living with me in the Grotty Hovel. Perhaps George had not told her. She had been ill for years before she died. I hoped her money would smooth the path for George and Sharon to settle down together.

The four of us sat down at a table in the middle of the courtyard and Rohan handed out copies of the menu. Sharon declined hers. She took out the one I had given her and I noticed she had crossed out things and made notes on them.

'Did you see the kitchen?' said Rohan, twirling his black moustache. 'It's perfect.'

'That's easy for you to say,' said Kieron. 'Where am I going to make the sushi?'

'We won't be having any sushi,' said Sharon, drawing her eyebrows together. 'My family isn't big on raw fish.'

'I'm not sure George's lot would be keen either to be fair,' I said.

Kieron crossed his arms and pouted. I could feel a tantrum looming.

'What are you proposing?' he said.

Sharon shrugged.

'Paté and toast, followed by roast beef with all the trimmings. Some sort of pudding.'

'Spotted dick?' said Kieron.

Rohan sniggered.

'Or a tart?' he said, arching an eyebrow.

Sharon shot him a look that almost singed it off. I searched my memory for an old-fashioned dessert favourite more suitable to the congregation.

'What about a Pavlova?' I said, 'Or a lemon meringue pie?'

'Oo, retro,' said Rohan. 'I like it.'

'Not a bad idea. What flavour paté?' said Kieron.

'How about mackerel?' said Sharon.

'I love mackerel paté,' I said. 'It will be much easier to make than sushi in that kitchen.'

Kieron rubbed his chin.

'That's true. We could serve it with sesame biscuits.'

'What about the wine?' said Sharon.

'Joy and Ryan Wells at the Shanty pub have a supplier in France who can provide us with reasonably priced red and white wines. Are you planning on serving champagne?' I said, knowing the answer.

Sharon laughed.

'George would throw a fit. There's no point. Can they source some prosecco too?'

'I'm sure they can. I'll find out.'

'And the cake?' said Sharon.

'Ghita has loads of ideas, but you can talk to her about it.'

'I don't care really. I don't eat cake.'

'I'll ask George, shall I?'

'Can she make something portable? So that people can take a piece home if they want to?'

'I'm sure that's possible. I'll ask her to make some suggestions.'

A petite woman emerged from the women's toilet in the passageway, her face covered in a perfect layer of foundation and sharp wings painted onto her eyelids. She resembled Sharon sufficiently for me to recognise her as Theresa Hurley, Sharon's sister. I wondered how long it had taken her to get the finish on her face. She even had rosebud lips like a china doll. She sat at the table and appraised us one by one. Her gaze rested on me and she smirked.

'The ex-wife and the gay couple,' she said and cackled. 'This is like a soap opera.'

'And which one are you?' said Kieron. 'The ugly sister?'

Rohan put his hand up to shush him.

'Honestly, Theresa. Do you have to throw the cat among the pigeons every time?' said Sharon, bright spots of colour appearing on her cheeks. 'Apologise. Now.'

'I'm sorry. My mouth is faster than my brain. This situation is so bizarre.'

'What are you doing here anyway? Aren't you supposed to be paying our supplier?'

Theresa shrugged.

'I sent Fintan. Even he can hand over a wad of cash without too many problems.'

'Fintan? Are you mad? We need to stay in their good books until we pay their invoice.'

'Too late now. I don't suppose I can smoke in here,' said Theresa, digging in her handbag and pulling out a packet of Rothmans.

'Definitely not,' said Rohan, wrinkling his face up in disgust.

'We were finished anyway,' I said, standing up. 'I'll be in touch, Sharon.'

She nodded, struggling to keep her face neutral. I felt a little sorry for her. My sister Helen had always been condescending, but never aggressive. Theresa and Fintan were the business partners from hell.

Chapter 6

After the meeting at Tarton Manor House, Rohan and Kieron disappeared into the kitchen at Surfusion, only surfacing to cross the road to Second Home and try out varieties of paté and gravy on me and Mouse. They were totally absorbed in their work and had stopped fighting which gave Ghita a break. She had decided to make a cupcake tower using individual square cakes in paper cups, but all her attempts to make a small-scale model had ended in total collapse. We offered the individual flavours to our customers at the Vintage and were keeping a running tab on the most popular. I never thought I could eat too much cake, but it turned out to be possible.

George had soon found out about the cake tastings at the Vintage and popped in most mornings for a coffee. He had become increasingly agitated by the cost of the wedding and the prospect of becoming a father again. Mouse made himself scarce during these visits, polishing tables downstairs or scrolling on his phone at the cash register. He found it hard to hear George talk about the new baby. I think George's attitude made it harder. I heard Mouse muttering 'another unwanted child' as he stalked downstairs.

To my surprise, Helen took George to task for his attitude. She often came to the shop to help me while her broken marriage went through its awful stages of dissolution. I wasn't at all sure how she would cope with being a single working woman again. However, George did not demure when she scolded him for complaining, telling him that a woman's wedding day should be one of the best days of her life, not an ode to the penny scrimpers and savers of life. I'm sure I heard her tell him to suck it up. He had gazed at her with admiration after one of these lectures. George still had the boarding school boy's fantasy of being bossed around by matron and Helen certainly fitted that bill. She was only a year older than me, but she lived in the 1950s. They had that in common.

Despite my reservations, Sharon also turned up at the Vintage to review the preparations for the wedding. I needn't have worried about her coveting my corner of the world. She took one look at the contents of the shop and then marched upstairs to get a coffee without the slightest curiosity. I hadn't planned on getting her a wedding present anyway, but I felt tempted to give her a 1970s neon lampshade to wreck the beige heaven of George's villa. Ghita quivered with anticipation as Sharon arrived. She had placed all the favoured flavours of cupcake on a tray and could barely contain her excitement. Sharon curled her lip at the delicacies.

'I don't eat cake,' she said. 'Just use the most popular flavours.'

Ghita deflated like a party balloon. I could feel disappointment seeping from her pores, but Sharon seemed oblivious.

'Where's the food then? Weren't we going to try it too?'

'I'll get Rohan to bring it over if you like, but he wanted to show you the restaurant,' said Ghita.

'I don't have time for that. I have to get an order out today.'

Ghita disappeared down the stairs and I watched her cross the road to Surfusion. She wiped her face with her sleeve, making my heart ache for her. All that work. Sharon had no heart.

Rohan didn't fare much better, but at least his food got the thumbs up. I could only imagine Kieron's tantrum if Sharon had rejected it. Even the lemon meringue pies were approved. At least Ghita got the credit for the lemon filling. A little smile crept across her face when Sharon licked her finger clean. For a person who didn't eat cake, she hoovered up the lemon meringue pie quick enough.

After she had swept out again, I squeezed Ghita's hand.

'Sorry about that. She's unappreciative at the best of times.'

'George is welcome to her,' she said. 'They deserve each other.'

I'm not sure how I managed to keep on track with all the disparate requirements of a relatively simple ceremony and after party. When I finished dealing with one issue, another arose. I received a hundred texts a day about favours, place settings, napkins, flowers, gravy, portion sizes, wine, and even one about vows from George. Honestly. Vows. As if I could help him with that. I gave up asking Sharon as she didn't seem to care about any of it. She only wanted a wedding to show off to her family, who were not keen on her marrying a police officer as half of them had police records for one thing or another. The more I found out about them, the greater my concern for the mess George had got himself into. How would he deal with one of his in-laws being arrested? The conflict of interests involved boggled my mind.

I tried not to contaminate Mouse with my misgivings, but my hacker stepson soon found out all he needed to know about them. He tried to hide it from me, but his poker face needed work. Fintan Hurley had a list of convictions as long as his arm, and a citation for violent behaviour, dismissed when the claimant didn't turn up in court. Even Theresa had had a brush with the law for deception. No wonder Sharon had her hands full. I wondered why she had worked in a police station. Perhaps it gave her access to useful inside information and lots of willing victims.

Despite Mouse's resistance, the idea of having a baby brother had sneaked past his defences, and I even caught him looking at sailing boat mobiles to hang above the cot. I wished I believed he would get a look in with his new sibling. Perhaps he could babysit, as neither George nor Sharon showed any signs that they would stay at home with the baby when it arrived. George had accepted his fate as the father to be, but the likelihood of him being hands on was slim. For Sharon the pregnancy was a golden ticket, but she never talked about the baby as a human creature who would soon invade her life and change it forever. I couldn't get my head around her complete lack of interest in it. It takes all sorts, but this felt like a disaster waiting to happen. I had told George I wouldn't be taking the baby in, like I had with Mouse, but I had lied to myself too. Mouse and I were as broody as a pair of chickens.

As the day for the wedding drew near, an unreal calm settled over us. Everything had gone without a hitch which made me nervous. I hadn't seen Harry for days and couldn't go to the flower market with him after I got a doctor's appointment the same day. Roz deputised for me. I had a pang of jealousy as they drove off together squabbling over which cassette to listen to. I went down to the wind shelter near my house to feed Herbert the seagull and sulk. The tide had gone out, leaving a vast expanse of beach with strips of sand and patches of rock pools. Several hardy residents leaned into the wind and slogged along the shore with their ecstatic dogs.

Helen's face appeared around the side of the shelter, peeping out of a bright yellow sou'wester jacket.

'I thought you'd be here,' she said.

She always impressed me with the way she could read my moods. Despite spending many years apart, she only needed the smallest of clues. In this case, Mouse had told her I had left the house looking miserable and she had immediately made for the wind shelter, knowing I'd be telling my troubles to Herbert.

'Who else is going to feed Herbert?' I said, patting the bench beside me.

'You could've said no to doing the wedding,' she said. 'George doesn't deserve any loyalty from you.'

'No, I couldn't. Mouse needs his father.'

'And what do you need?'

'I've got Harry, and Mouse, and Hades. And now you too, again. That's more than enough.'

'I'm flattered. Do you think George should be marrying this woman?' she said, surprising me with the question.

'She's preggers, so, yes, I do.'

Helen shook her head and tutted.

'I meant, are they suited? She seems sort of brassy and common.'

I laughed, startling the ravens who had inched closer hoping for some stale toast. Helen had always been a snob.

'That's not very charitable of you. I'm sure she has redeeming qualities too.'

'Well hidden,' said Helen.

She had gone pink, which struck me as odd. I pulled her around to see her expression, but she could not look me in the eye. The penny dropped.

'Oh, my goodness. You like him, you like George.'

'What? No, of course I don't. How could you even suggest such a thing.'

'Because you're heating up the wind shelter with that blush.'

'I'm not blushing. It's the menopause. A hot flush.'

'No, it isn't. You borrowed a Tampax from me last week.'

'Perimenopause then. Stop being ridiculous. As if.'

I smiled at her use of the teenage phrase. Olivia had left her mark on her mother.

'Okay, but you're way too late. You'll have to wait for the inevitable divorce.'

'Inevitable? It must be hard for you to see them together.'

'Not really.'

'And the baby?'

I bit my lip.

'That's harder.'

'You could still have a baby, with Harry, if you wanted to.'

'Theoretically. I'm not even sure I want one. And there's Mouse.'

'True. He might feel outnumbered if we all started having babies, poor lamb.'

'It's hard enough already. I don't want him to panic.'

'Isn't the wedding this weekend?'

I sighed.

'I'm afraid so, but I think we'll be ready somehow.'

'You can do this. One final effort and you'll be free of George for good.'

'Let's hope so.'

Chapter 7

I hadn't wanted to attend the wedding, but Mouse insisted that Harry and I accompany him there, or he wouldn't go either. I sympathised. At his age I would rather have run naked down the high street than endure an 'old people's wedding' with all that entailed. I hoped there would be other people his age so they could all scroll on their phones together and complain about compulsory family fun. George had agreed to Harry coming as well, so we were a self-contained unit should we find ourselves in hostile territory. Being a firm believer in the phrase, everything that can go wrong will go wrong, I chose to wear a practical, green, velvet trouser suit I had purchased for work from Jigsaw, my favourite shop for working clothes back in the days. I increased the glamour by adding strings of 1930s amber and Bakelite beads and some high-heeled leather boots.

When the day came, I couldn't resist a trip to the local hairdresser. Marge Dawson's eyes lit up when she saw me. She couldn't wait to regale me with the full download on her wedding to Reg Dolan.

'Only thirty years late. But it's thanks to you. And Delia is doing much better now. Reg dotes on her.'

I didn't need to contribute more than a nod and a smile as she filled me in on the details while she sculpted my hair into a gorgeous beehive. When she had finished, I looked as if I had stepped out of a B52 video. Mouse stared open-mouthed at me when I collected him at the Grotty Hovel. He didn't look so bad himself. He had the looks of a medieval prince with his shiny black curls, bow lips and sad grey eyes. The vintage suit with drainpipe trousers made him look taller. We were ready for our close up for a 1950s movie with Spencer Tracy and Katherine Hepburn.

'I hope this isn't as awful as I think it's going to be,' he said.

'It will be much, much worse, but think of the fun we'll have reliving it later.'

He grinned.

'Now you put it that way.'

I crossed my fingers it wouldn't be as bad as I imagined. I had put my heart and soul into making Sharon's and George's day a good one. I couldn't deny I still cared about George, despite his selfish nature. After all, I had loved him once for a reason, and he hadn't changed much. I was the one who had changed, and I felt magnanimous in my freedom. My father always told me to be the better person and I guess it rubbed off on me.

A knock on the door heralded the arrival of Harry, who looked dapper in his suit and highly polished shoes. You can take the man out of the army, but you can't take the army out of the man. Even his bald pate shone. His pupils dilated when he sniffed me and admired my hair.

'You look good enough to eat,' he said. 'Are we ready to give away the groom?'

Mouse laughed.

'Give him away? We're paying her to take him,' I said.

'Are you next?' said Mouse.

'I already asked her,' said Harry. 'Tanya doesn't like to be rushed.'

He pulled me in for a kiss. I tapped him on the nose with my lipstick.

'Okay, but last one. I've got to put on my lips.'

'Honestly, you guys should stop messing about and move in together,' said Mouse, opening the front door and stopping Hades from sauntering out with us. 'You can't come. Cats and weddings don't mix.'

If cats could glare, I'd swear Hades swept us all with a magnificent one. He stalked to the back door and let himself out, vanishing into the brambles.

'Remind me to buy some secateurs,' I said. 'We really need to attack that back garden before the spring.'

'So you keep saying,' said Mouse. 'I'll believe it when I see it.'

'There might be treasure buried in there.'

'Or bodies. Perhaps you should just leave it as it is,' said Harry. 'Stop procrastinating. We need to be there first to make sure it all goes smoothly.'

As always, when faced with a challenging day, the presence of Harry made me feel braver and ready for anything. I had seen the seating plan and I knew I had been placed at the odds and sods table with all the leftovers. Not that I blamed Sharon. Who could be more leftover than her husband's ex-wife?

I did not go into the church as I felt more than entitled to skip that part of the service. I waited in the car for half an hour and then I put on my winter coat and walked to the main entrance of the church. A stone buttress offered me sanctuary out of sight while I waited for people to emerge and I confess to having a sneaky cigarette from a packet of ten which I had bought to help me through the day. Only one, I promise. As I sucked in the smoke and enjoyed the high after such a long time without a cigarette, it took all my discipline to stub it out before I reached the butt. As I searched in my clutch bag for my breath mints, the church door opened and I shrunk back into the crevice to avoid detection. The sound of a lighter broke the silence and the distinctive smell of a Rothmans cigarette wafted around the corner. Then Theresa Hurley's distinctive nasal voice cut through the frigid air.

'I can't believe she got him down the aisle. You've got to hand it to her.'

'He's not much cop as a detective, is he?' A man's voice. Fintan?

'Ha bloody ha. You think you're such a comedian. Well, that's phase two accomplished. Please try and be polite to George. It's not for much longer.'

'I won't rock the boat, but it better be worth it. She hasn't convinced me lately.'

'Don't worry. She'll come good and take him for everything he's got.'

They both snorted and took a few more pulls on their cigarettes. The sun had gone down and I shivered despite my thick coat. I heard the crunch of shoes on the gravel as they stamped on their cigarette ends.

'We'd better get back inside. They'll be coming out of the vestry soon after signing the certificate.'

'Excellent. I'm freezing my arse off here and I'm fecking hungry.'

'You're always hungry.'

'Get in there.'

I stood frozen to the spot, not only by the cold. Sharon's love of the good life had been apparent from day one, but I had been under the illusion, like most people we knew, that she genuinely liked George and wanted to marry him. I walked away from the church, taking the footpath that led directly to Tarton Manor House instead of waiting for Harry and Mouse. I craved time and space to mull over what I had just heard. I also needed my head on straight to deal with the next phase of the wedding. The ground had begun to freeze, and I could feel it crackle under my boots. The leafless trees loomed overhead and some rooks fought among their sodden black branches. Panic had gripped me in its chilly embrace. What on earth should I do?

I entered the hall through the back door leading into the kitchens and bumped into Rohan whose friendly smile froze on his face as he took in my shocked state. He hurried me into the kitchen and stood me beside the ovens, rubbing my hands between his and shouting at the sous chef to make me a hot toddy. I sipped it as warmth returned to my body, trying to digest what I had heard. I certainly couldn't tell Rohan, but he misinterpreted my distress.

'It's all been too much for you, hasn't it?' he said, rolling his eyes at Kieron who stood to one side his hands on his hips. He shook his head, but the frustration that somebody would invade his kitchen at such a crucial moment oozed out of his pores.

'My fault entirely,' I said. 'I should never have agreed to take on this gig.'

'You're rid of him now.'

The sound of stilettos alerted me to the arrival of the wedding party at the conservatory. I took a deep breath and kissed Rohan on the cheek. Then I removed my coat, folding it over my arm.

'I'm feeling much calmer now. Thanks for the warm up.'

I hung the coat on a hook in the passageway and entered the conservatory which had filled with feather fascinators like a cage of exotic birds. Nearly every single woman wore one to go with their outfit. Vivid silk jumpsuits were all the rage and many women had chosen to wear one with long necklaces or chokers. Multicoloured feathers on the fascinators flickered and bounced under the lights. The local milliner must have mass produced them. The sound of women competing to compliment each other on their outfits in loud voices rose to a crescendo. I once saw a flock of flamingos rush up to a feeding station all squawking at once which sounded remarkably similar. The scent of perfume filled the air as many fragrances mixed to produce a heady brew which made me slightly nauseous. I hoped Sharon had been judicious with the choice of tables for the more flamboyant members of the flock, or feathers could fly after a few glasses of prosecco.

The room itself looked fantastic with the lights on the chandeliers bouncing off the windows and causing every piece of metal in the room to twinkle. I had gone for white tablecloths with simple, pink-rose centrepieces, and avoided the Christmas theme altogether. Wedding favours sat on the side plates; twee silver bookmarks with a silhouette of a kissing couple. The uncharitable thought that they could be reused danced through my mind. I glanced at the entrance and caught sight of George in the receiving line. Usually that sort of thing was right up his street. He could be charming when required and had a good line of patter, but he had a face like thunder. I couldn't remember ever seeing him looking so livid. Sharon had shrunk inside her dress and her white face was almost the same colour. What on earth had happened? Had he found out the same thing I had?

But I didn't have time to dwell on this peculiar sight. People needed to be shepherded away from the receiving line and over to their tables. I positioned myself at the board with the seating map and pointed people to their allotted seats. There were eruptions of glee from some and pursing of lips from others as they discovered their fate. I tried not to glance at George again, but his rigid stance and thunderous brow told me all I needed to know. Something had gone horribly wrong in the vestry.

Chapter 8

Once everyone had entered the conservatory and the conversation had calmed at the tables, I made my way to my designated table. I took another glance at George who had half turned away from Sharon and conversed in whispers with Mouse whose face mirrored George's. Seeing George and Mouse all alone on the top table made me realise how isolated George was. No wonder he couldn't drop me totally. I was the only link back to his parents and his past life. He had Mouse and me, and nobody else. Sharon didn't count after the conversation I heard outside the church. I had already prepared myself for telling George the truth in the near future, after the wedding had finished. I couldn't let her get away with this. Somehow, I had to get through the dinner first.

I sat at my table and looked around. Normally the odds and sods table is placed as far away from the bridal top table as possible. Ours sat in the corner between the toilet block and the kitchens. As an ex-journalist, this was more of a bonus than a punishment as I could observe all the comings and goings and pick up snippets of gossip as women entered and emerged from the toilets. As darkness set in, cheeks became rosier and giggling louder. I could see Mouse at the top table, his eyebrows drawn together in frustration as the adults around him asked him what he considered to be stupid questions. I caught his eye and pulled up the corners of my mouth with my fingers. He snorted, but his face relaxed and he leant in to listen to a question from George.

We were definitely a bit Liquorice All Sorts on my table. I told myself brides have better things to think about than their eccentric aunties, an alcoholic single friend, an 'uncle' or friend of the family who had paedophile tendencies, and her husband's ex-wife who would rather squeeze lemon juice into her eyeballs than attend. So why not lump all your problem guests at one table? If you are a single woman of a certain age, you almost invariably end up there. They assign you to the weirdo table and you wish you could be at home watching Rizzoli and Isles, and eating that tin of shortbread you bought in M&S when you went in for a new bra. That sinking feeling when you looked at each other and know why you're there. That horrible embarrassment of knowing you're extra and no one wants to sit with you. And if everyone is odd except you, maybe it's you that's odd. Meanwhile, at the normal tables, the young folk are all looking at their mobile phones, and the middle-aged couples at each other's partners and wondering if that outfit used to fit before the menopause.

Harry raised his eyebrows at me from the other side of the table where two stick thin women with beaky noses were telling him their life stories. I guessed they were sisters. He did a good job pretending to be fascinated and the excitement of having a handsome man all to themselves shone from their faces. I loved him even more at that moment. The young waiter arrived at the table with a tray of mackerel paté and a selection of toasted brioche. I greeted the food with undisguised joy as I had only had a stale Weetabix for breakfast and my stomach had started to dissolve itself with hunger. I had not noticed the man beside me, but his cheap suit and shiny face rang a bell as he leaned in to whisper in my ear.

'Fancy meeting you here,' he said. 'I like a woman with an appetite. Turns me on.'

To my horror I realised I had met him before at the house of fleas, a revolting clearance Harry and I had done where the carpets were alive with the critters. I flashed a plea for help across the table to Harry, but he had all his attention on the beaky sisters and did not notice my plight.

'What did you say your name was?' I said.

'Ray Colthard. I'm sure you remember stripping for me at my grandparent's cottage?'

'What I remember is my boyfriend wanting to beat you up. The one with all the muscles across the table from us.'

Colthard's eyebrows rose almost off his forehead and he turned hastily to the woman on his other side, leaving me to chat to a man I took to be Methuselah's brother. He appeared to be at least five hundred years old and deaf as a post, but he had a lovely smile which showed off his dentures to perfection. They were the kind of spare teeth that swam around his mouth like goldfish in a bowl while he tried to keep them under control. I couldn't make head or tail of anything he said, but I smiled back and ate my paté and a spare portion left over by Vicky, a vegan teenager sitting on the other side of Methuselah. I couldn't imagine why she had not been seated at the youngster's table, and seemed to be something to do with the mortuary. She had so many piercings that her ears had become shredded and she had started in on her eyebrows which looked red and swollen. I called over the waiter and told him to get our vegan starter from Rohan. She gave me a lovely smile and started to tell me about making up dead people so they looked fabulous at their funerals. I relaxed a little. I couldn't let the things I'd overheard ruin the wedding. They would keep.

After the main course, the hot toddy I had gulped down had worked its way to my bladder and I excused myself to go to the toilet. I headed for the rather glamorous bathrooms in the small block connecting the conservatory to the main house. On my way, I noticed a man lurking near the swinging doors which led to the main building. He did not acknowledge me, but stared fixedly out at the wedding, his brow furrowed. I decided to ignore him and entered the women's toilet instead. The walls were painted a soothing dove grey and a lavender diffuser sat between the sinks.

Once inside, I entered one of the stalls and wiped the seat before sitting on it and taking some deep breaths. The aroma of lavender had an immediate effect. I could feel myself relax and I lingered a while to recover my good humour. I hoped George had managed to calm down too. I stood up and reached for the door handle, when I heard voices and saw high heels enter the bathroom. One woman wore a silk jumpsuit, or trousers, and the other a wedding dress. I recognised the voices immediately.

'You told him? Are you out of your mind?'

'He has a right to know. He can't back out now anyway.'

'Yes, he can. He can annul the marriage if he wants to. How do you know he won't?'

'He didn't even want the baby. I'm pretty sure he's more relieved than angry.'

'Does he know you faked the pregnancy?'

I almost gasped and had to clamp my jaw shut. How could things get any worse?

'I told him I lost it.'

'And he believes you?'

'I think so.'

'You'd better be right. We're relying on you to pull this off.'

'It's not going to work anyway. George isn't stupid.'

'Don't let Fintan hear you saying that.'

I waited about a minute after they left before exiting, and then re-entered the fray. The mixture of noise and shock made me feel quite light headed and I stood swaying outside the bathroom trying to regain my equilibrium. Suddenly, Theresa was at my side. She grabbed hold of my arm with bony fingers.

'Were you in the bathroom just now?' she said.

'What? No, I went to check something with the main house reception. Why do you ask?'

'I saw you outside the church too. I hope you weren't spying on us.'

'This may amaze you, but I didn't fancy watching my ex-husband marry your sister. I had a cigarette outside. I didn't even see you there.'

She looked into my face for signs I might be lying, but my face was already flushed from drink and I held her stare.

'You'd better not be lying,' she said. 'We're not good with snitches down our way.'

She let go of my arm and walked back to the top table where she whispered aggressively into Fintan's ear. He narrowed his eyes and drew his finger across his throat. I almost fainted. Somebody put their hand on my shoulder and I jumped out of my skin. Sharon stood there grinning.

'Nice suit,' she said. 'I've got a surprise for you. Wait for me here below the women's changing room in about five minutes.'

Before I could answer, she'd gone again. I made my way to the table and poured myself a glass of water. I gulped it down and tried to calm myself as the inner tables were moved back and people crowded around to see the first dance. There was no sign of either George or Sharon, so after a short, confused pause, couples spilled onto the floor and began to dance together. Mouse appeared behind me and offered me his hand. I shook my head, but he ignored me and pulled me upright.

'We have to talk,' he said. 'Now.'

'Does George know about Sharon and the phantom baby?' I said.

'How did you…? Never mind. Yes, he's hysterical. I sent him to the men's changing room to calm down.'

'I wish that were the only problem. I overhead the Walshes discussing how Sharon had planned this all along.'

Mouse swore under his breath.

'What are we going to do?'

'I'd like you to dance with Vicky,' I whispered, pointing at her back. 'Sharon asked me to meet her at the loos in a minute.'

'What does she want?'

'I'm not sure, but nothing sinister. She was tiddly and giggly. Maybe she bought me a present for organising the wedding. That would be a normal thing to do.'

'There's nothing normal about this wedding,' said Mouse. 'Be careful. Sharon's family is nuts.'

He tapped Vicky on the shoulder and she turned around. Her face lit up with pleasure when he asked her to dance and she bounced out of her seat. I watched them head for the dance floor. Mouse loved to dance and so, it seemed, did she. They were soon cutting a dash. Harry made signs at me across the table, but I shook my head and mouthed 'in a minute'. Then I headed back to the passageway where the toilets and changing rooms were situated. As I got closer, I noticed an odd shape on the floor. My heart almost stopped in fright when I recognised it as a person, and even more weirdly, someone wearing the same green trouser suit as me. She could have been my clone. I gently turned her over. She moaned and open her eyes.

'Surprise,' said Sharon, and then she closed them again.

Blood pooled under her head and I tried not to touch it as I took her pulse. The whole world seemed slip into slow motion. I looked around in disbelief and saw that one of the gargoyle flower pots had detached from the balcony outside the men's changing room and plummeted to the ground. It must have hit Sharon as she exited the staircase from the women's changing room. As I crouched dazed over her body, George's face appeared above me on the men's balcony.

'What on earth is going on down there, Sharon?' he said. 'Oh my God, has something happened to Tanya?'

'I'm Tanya,' I said. 'I'm afraid there's been a terrible accident. Sharon's dead. You need to call Brighton.'

Chapter 9

Poor George. I watched his face as he tried to digest the fact that his bride had died a few hours after their vows to part only at death. He staggered down the steps from the changing room and knelt awkwardly on the ground beside Sharon, stopping himself from pitching forward with his hands. A broad smile had frozen on Sharon's features, giving her a macabre air. Her auburn curls were matted with blood. I couldn't believe how she had transformed so fast from giggling bride to empty shell. George touched my arm.

'You need to move away now,' he said. 'This may be a crime scene.'

He looked up at the balcony where a gap marked the spot from where the gargoyle pot had fallen. I couldn't help noticing he had concrete dust on his hands. He must have got it on them when he knelt down to look at the body, because the alternative did not bear thinking about. He saw me looking at them and wiped them on his suit.

'Poor quality,' he said. 'Not stone, but concrete moulds.'

I didn't have time to speculate on his weird reaction to Sharon's death before a scream rang out from behind me, and I turned to see Theresa and Fintan running towards us. I held up my hands to prevent them coming into the passageway and contaminating the crime scene.

Pretty soon, I was holding the whole wedding party at bay. I've got to hand it to George. As soon as he realised what had happened, he made the officers who were at the event cordon off the passageway with a line of chairs and stand guard over it. Then he called Brighton police station and asked them to send D.I. Antrim and the Scene of Crime Officers (SOCO) crew immediately to attend a possible suspicious death. Mouse stood beside Theresa Hurley at the front of the crowd, his mouth open. She turned on him, furious with grief.

'Your father did this,' she said. 'Look at him. He didn't have the sense to leave the scene of the crime. He'll go down for years.'

I shook my head at Mouse, but his face had creased in fear and he looked as if he might cry. Vicky hung on to his arm like a drowning woman, her mascara running down one pale cheek making her look like Pierrot. Then Harry pushed his way through the crowd and put his arm around Mouse's shoulder. He steered him away from the scene and back towards the tables. I could see Mouse gesticulating and resisting, but not many people were stronger than Harry. The knowledge Mouse would be safe with him gave me a grain of relief. Meanwhile, George wore his poker face, but behind his calm façade his mind must have been whirring. I caught him staring at me several times as if trying to read my expression, the way I tried to read his. The coincidence of George being in the men's changing room on the same balcony from where the gargoyle pot had fallen had not escaped me. I had seen his naked fury when he found out about Sharon and her fake pregnancy. But then I remembered that Mouse had told me he had sent George to the room to calm down. He couldn't have known Sharon would be there too. The man I knew would never select murder as a solution to a problem. George had many faults, but he had a strong moral compass which would not have allowed him to do it.

People started to drift away from the cordon and exclamations of dismay could be heard as P.C. Joe Brennan did a circuit of the tables, informing people they could not leave yet. He was almost unrecognisable in his smart suit. A breathless Carol Burns, dressed in a skintight velour catsuit which made her look like a short, plump salami, helped him to restore order. As a result of the unrest, either Rohan or Kieron made the decision to send out the waiters with the lemon meringue tartlets. Quite a few people took the option of having dessert 'since we're here anyway'. The magnificent wedding cake of exquisite cupcakes sat alone on the top table, abandoned and untasted. Ghita had planned for everyone to take one home each, but touching them would almost have been blasphemous. I had anticipated a trainwreck at the wedding, but this topped everything.

And then Detective Inspector Terry Antrim stalked into the conservatory with his SOCO team following behind him. He wore a dinner jacket and bowtie which made him resemble a heron more than ever as he picked his way across the floor. He stopped at the cordon and gazed at the scene, taking in the body on the floor, and George and me in our own private hells standing to one side. He raised an eyebrow when he spotted me and a smirk passed his thin lips. George galvanised himself and approached the cordon, but D.I. Antrim held up his hand.

'Don't come out, George. The SOCO team will need to take your suit and test your hands for residues. The same for you, Mrs Carter.'

'But I've got nothing to do with this. And I'm not Mrs Carter. She is,' I said pointing at Sharon. 'My name is Tanya Bowe.'

'That's what they all say. I bet you weren't jealous or resentful either. What kind of woman would come to her ex-husband's wedding anyway?'

He guffawed, and pointed us out to the team. We had to go through the ignominy of changing into white SOCO suits and foot covers and put all our clothes into evidence bags.

'Why are you wearing the same clothes as the victim?' said the young woman taking samples from my hands and nails in the ladies' toilet. 'Isn't that a bit creepy?'

I wondered if she realised women my age shopped in chain stores like she did. Or did she think we just went to charity shops and thrift stores and bought second-hand clothes? I shrugged and pulled on the foot covers.

'I have no idea. She was wearing a wedding dress last time I saw her. She must have changed into her leaving outfit. These velvet suits were all the rage at one time.'

'In the stone age, you mean?' she said, smirking. 'I don't suppose Terry noticed you're wearing the same outfit as a dead woman. I'll have to tell him.'

I couldn't believe she called him Terry. I wondered if D.I. Antrim would approve of such disrespect. Then a shiver ran down my spine. Did anyone know Sharon had the same suit as me? Probably not. It wasn't like a green velvet trouser suit was commonplace. Most women seemed to wear black, even to parties where they looked like a flock of flightless crows. The fashion for these suits was at least ten years old too. Everyone at the wedding had seen me wearing the green trouser suit. Had someone meant me harm instead of Sharon?

By the time we emerged, the paramedic had certified Sharon as deceased and SOCOs were taking photographs and laser measurements of the scene around the body. It couldn't have been more surreal. The wedding had morphed into a murder in an instant. I watched as one of them took a sample of the blood on the floor. It had already coagulated, and the Q tip made a channel through it, making me feel nauseous. They had taken away the gargoyle flower pot. It had left an impact mark on the ground which reminded me of the dust pattern left when birds flew into a window. The large and comforting figure of Flo Barrington, the forensic consultant, bent over the body in a tight SOCO suit. Her mane of grey streaked hair had been stuffed into the hood, and her finery fought the seams of the coverall. She looked up as we approached. A wry smile crept across her face.

'We look like the telly tubbies,' she said. 'We must stop meeting like this. I'm so sorry about Sharon. It's a real shock for the D.I. He'll need your support, you know. We'll be finished here soon and we'll take the body away. Then the SOCO can get stuck in upstairs.'

George did not react to the activity around him. He folded and unfolded his arms as if he didn't know where to put them. His eyes had glazed over with shock. D.I. Antrim who had waited outside the cordon while the forensic officer and SOCOs did their jobs, beckoned me with his finger. I followed him into the main hotel where he had requisitioned a meeting room on the ground floor for interrogations. The hotel had put up some decorative screens to make cubicles and he ushered me into one of them. He had a digital recorder with him and he spoke into it to confirm the date and time and place of the recording. I stood uncertain in my SOCO suit, wishing the ground would swallow me up.

'Sit down,' he said. 'Before you fall down. Would you like a glass of water?'

D.I. treating me kindly was the last thing I expected and it broke my resistance quicker than any sarcastic comment. To my intense embarrassment I burst into floods of tears and he had to find a tissue to combat the flow of mucus issuing from my nostrils. He did not speak, but waited patiently until I regained some semblance of control over my emotions.

'Okay?' he said.

I sniff and nodded at him.

'Not really. It's pretty shocking. Especially…'

'Especially what?'

'We were wearing the same suit in the same colour. We've always looked similar, but I felt as if it were me lying on the ground. I can't explain it.'

D.I. Antrim made a note on his tablet. He rubbed his chin.

'Have you been threatened at all?'

'No. Not at all, but something happened today which scared me. I'm probably just being stupid.'

'Your instincts are not in question here. If you felt in danger, you may be right. I want you to tell me exactly what happened today. Leave nothing out.'

'Do you mean since I arrived at the wedding?'

'For now. I'd like to get your recollections of the whole event while they're still fresh. We can go into the background in our next interview.'

I told him about the wedding from start to finish, including the conversations I'd overheard at the church about the intended swindle of George, and Sharon's false pregnancy, and Fintan's gesture at me. I struggled to give a clear picture of the murder scene, but I remembered not to include any opinions I had of the events. When I described George's face appearing on the balcony, my deep shock must have been apparent as I could hardly get the words out.

'How well do you know your ex-husband, Ms Bowe?' he said.

'Better than he knows himself,' I said. 'We used to be soulmates.'

'Do you think he killed Sharon Walsh?'

I shook my head.

'There's no chance. My George would never have considered such a thing. He's more law abiding than anyone I've ever met. He's quite infuriating, actually.'

I managed a smile.

'My George? He's not yours anymore, is he? How long have you been divorced?'

'I meant the George I knew. We've been divorced a year or so.'

'Why did you divorce?'

'He met Sharon. It's a long story. Can I tell you tomorrow? I organised the wedding and I'm so exhausted.'

His eyebrows flew up.

'You organised your ex-husband's wedding?'

I nodded.

'I wanted him to be happy. His son lives with me and he needs his father. We were trying to be civilised.'

He stared hard at me for an instant, and I felt as if I had been pierced to the core by lasers.

'Did George know she had faked her pregnancy?'

I swallowed.

'I heard her tell Theresa she had confessed about losing the baby to George. She didn't tell him she had faked it from the beginning.'

'Before or after the ceremony.'

'After. In the vestry.'

'Did George want the baby?'

'You'll have to ask him that.'

'We're finished here. I'll text you a time to come to the station. We need to work our way through the other guests first. I expect we'll interview the main suspects at Seacastle station to keep the investigation nearer to the site of the murder, if it was a murder.'

'They're not really suspects yet, are they?'

'All of you are, until I say otherwise.'

Chapter 10

George turned up at the Grotty Hovel the next morning while we were still in our pyjamas. He rang the doorbell with a timid buzz, unlike his usual long blast, so it surprised me to find him there, diminished and dishevelled.

'Can I come in?' he said.

'Of course. Where have you come from?'

'The cells.'

'What? Did D.I. Antrim lock you up?'

'No, I asked him for permission to sleep there. I couldn't go home, because they may treat it as a crime scene.'

His voice shook and his eyes were pools of pain and confusion. My heart broke for him. Nobody deserves that sort of misery.

'Sit down and I'll get you a cup of sea,' I said, trying to stay calm.

Grey with tiredness, George walked over and sank onto the sofa. He looked as if he might burst into tears. Just then, Mouse came down the stairs two at a time.

'Are we due at the police station yet?' he said. 'I can hardly believe what happened—'

Then he spotted George on the sofa. Mouse's face crumpled as George stood up to greet him. He went straight to George and enveloped him in a hug. A raw sob such as I had never heard before emerged from

George's throat. I felt like an intruder on their moment and went to hide in the kitchen where I made a big pot of tea mixed with tears. I had never seen George demonstrate any feelings for Mouse before and it hurt my heart to see them connect. I heard footsteps on the stairs and Harry appeared in the kitchen, his eyes wide.

'They're crying out there,' he said.

'I know. Would you like a cup of tea?'

'I'm traumatised. I'd like a hug first. Are you okay? How's George taking Sharon's death?'

'We haven't discussed the wedding yet.'

'It's surreal. Poor old George. No happy ending for him.'

I had not told Harry about George's mixed feelings about the baby and the wedding. Harry saw life in black and white. I couldn't shift him easily when he took sides and I wanted him to be on George's. He let go of me and took some cups from the cupboard, loading up a tray with the tea things. We emerged to find Mouse and George on the sofa. Mouse had his arm around George's shoulders and Hades had jumped into George's lap where he stroked him absentmindedly. Harry shook George's hand and poured cups of tea for everyone. He had taken a hands-off approach with my other cases, but, strange as it seems, he had a protective attitude towards George. I wondered if George represented a surrogate for his estranged brother Nick, but I had never asked him. I still hoped Harry and Nick could bridge their divide, no matter how wide it seemed to them. Harry took a large swig of tea and wiped the drips off his chin with his pyjama sleeve.

'How did it go with D.I. Antrim?' he said.

'He interviewed me under caution,' said George.

'Under caution? Was that necessary?' I said.

'I'd have done the same to him,' said George. 'I'm a prime suspect.'

'What did he ask you?' said Mouse.

'He wanted to know what I was doing upstairs. I told him I had gone to the men's changing room to cool down after…'

He trailed off and looked at Mouse.

'After Sharon told him about the non-existent baby,' said Mouse.

'We know about the baby,' I said. 'I heard Sharon and Theresa discuss it in the loo.'

'So, you know how she deceived me? I would never have married her otherwise. She lied and lied. I told him how she had tricked me into marrying her.'

'I don't suppose that helped much,' I said.

'I told him the truth. He'll find out anyway. There's no point lying. Antrim asked me if I had pushed the gargoyle off the balcony to scare her and killed her by mistake. I told him I hadn't left the room until I heard a loud noise outside in the passageway.'

'Did he interview anyone else?'

'I don't think so. Sharon's family were too shocked.'

The doorbell rang again making us all jump.

'Who on earth is that?' I said.

Harry went to open it, still in his dressing gown, but then George was the only one dressed at that stage. Helen stood at the door, breathing hard and bedraggled.

'I've just heard about the wedding. You poor things. What about George? Is he—'

I put my finger to my lips and flicked my eyes towards the sofa. Her startled glance alighted on George.

'Good heavens,' she said, and pushed past me, going straight over to him. 'You poor man. How utterly dreadful for you to lose your wife and unborn child in a horrible accident. You must be devastated.'

George opened his mouth to reply and shut it again. I pulled Helen into the kitchen.

'Ow, stop it. Why are you—'

'Who told you about this?' I said.

'Ghita rang me. Rohan told her about Sharon being killed by a falling flower pot.'

'I'm not sure how much she told you, but it's a lot more complicated than a simple accident. Sharon may have been murdered and George is a prime suspect.'

'But he wouldn't. He couldn't have. I don't believe it.'

'None of us do, sweety, but it doesn't look good for him. He found out Sharon lied about her pregnancy shortly before she died.'

'She lied? I can't believe it. I'd have been livid, but that's not a reason to kill someone. Divorce is easy these days.'

My practical sister. I almost smiled.

'The flower pot fell from the balcony where he had gone to calm down. D.I Antrim is investigating.'

'That horrid man. He'll pin it on George if he can. You've got to stop him.'

'That's not true. D.I. Antrim is a good policeman, even if we don't like him.'

'George doesn't stand a chance with D.I. Antrim on the case. You've got to help George. You'll find out who did it, won't you?'

'I'm not sure I can. D.I. Antrim's not going to give me any information if he can help it.'

'That's what you said last time, but you still found the killer. You're so talented at this. You should charge.'

'I think I charged George enough for the wedding already.'

She couldn't help laughing.

'You're going to help then.'

'Of course, I am.'

She beamed.

'In that case, I'm going to help too.'

I raised an eyebrow at this offer. Helen suffered from gullibility due to her lack of imagination concerning people's motives. I couldn't imagine her being much help in a murder investigation. She waited for me to answer and I dreaded hurting her feelings. But then I had a brain wave that would keep them both out of trouble, hopefully.

'I need all the help I can get,' I said. 'George is out on the street, you know, and he can't stay here. '

'Why not?'

'I found the body remember, and George is the prime suspect. If he moves in with me, D.I. Antrim will think we planned it.'

Helen swallowed and bit her lip.

'George can stay in my house. He can use Olivia's room.'

'Are you sure? It's a lot to ask.'

'I'm sure, but only if you promise to investigate.'

'What if George lost his temper and killed her by mistake?'

'I don't believe that. And neither do you.'

I rolled my eyes, but she was right. I'd have staked my life on it.

'Okay, I'll do my best.'

Chapter 11

George accepted Helen's offer to use Olivia's bedroom for the time being without quibble. I suspected he couldn't bear to go back to the beige villa, even if he were allowed. The flood of guilt and shame and fury he had experienced after Sharon's death had frightened him. George had never been great with feelings and he had been overwhelmed. Helen took him under her motherly wing and into her empty nest with tender care. Her nurturing skills would be key to getting him back on his feet again and I felt grateful somebody cared enough to help him.

Harry and I galvanised ourselves to return to Tarton Manor House that afternoon, as soon as we got the all clear from forensics. We drove over in the van followed by Rohan and Kieron who had left their utensils in the kitchen and the leftover food in the hotel's fridges and pantries. Harry's brow had been furrowed all morning. He had found George's distress palpable and it had upset him greatly.

'We must prove George innocent,' he said. 'He would never have murdered Sharon. He's not always kind, but there's no way he would have done this. It's completely out of character. Let me help you with this investigation. I can spot a killer. I've worked with men who loved to kill.'

'But what if it's a woman? Could you spot that too?'

He sighed.

'I don't know. But I need to help. George is my friend.'

'He's lucky to have you,' I said. 'I'm sure you can help me. The moral support is worth more than you can imagine on this case. It's hard to stay neutral.'

Harry's knuckles showed white on the steering wheel.

'He's free now, you know. When this is all over, I'd understand if—'

'If what? You silly man. I love you. We're going to help George together because he's Mouse's father and we believe in his integrity. He may be a bit of a shit, but he's our piece of excrement. Anyway, I believe my sister has a crush on him.'

'Helen? You're joking right.'

'I wish I was. She's always approved of him, but now she blushes when she's near him.'

'And you don't mind?'

'I absolutely don't. I know that's weird, but if they find happiness together, I will be glad. After all, I'm the cat who got the cream.'

Harry grinned.

'You know how to make me blush too. What shall we tackle first?'

'First, we've got to help the lads get all the food packaged up. We can take it to the Veterans' charity in Seacastle. They can freeze most of it and dole it out to people in need who come in from the cold.'

'Can we keep some cupcakes? I didn't get one last night.'

'Yes, but not where George can see them. I don't want him reminded of the wedding.'

'We could have them with a coffee in the Vintage.'

The conservatory stood bare and deserted in the weak afternoon light. The table tops formerly covered in crisp white linen tablecloths that skimmed the ground, and in settings of shining cutlery at each place, turned out to be pieces of bare plywood balanced on metal struts. Some streamers from party poppers lay on the floor, flattened and marked with heavy footprints. We entered the kitchen where Rohan and Kieron were removing food from the fridges and packaging it in tin foil. When they saw us enter, they moved on to sorting out their utensils from the drawers and drying boards. With four of us working diligently, it only took us an hour to clear up. Rohan and Kieron loaded up Harry's van with the food and put the utensils in theirs, before leaving us to finish up.

The hotel manager entered the kitchen and started to fuss and fret, picking things up and putting them down again for no good reason. He put his hands on his hips and tutted at us as if we were cluttering the place up with our presence. I had the strangest feeling of déjà vu like I had seen him before somewhere.

'Have you finished yet? I need to get the room ready for the next event. The forensic team wouldn't let us in yesterday.'

I read his name tag. Tim Boulting. He looked exactly like Ray Colthard, down to the shiny face. I knew where I had seen him before too; in the passageway during the wedding.

'The kitchen's clear, but I wondered if we might see the crime scene. I'm a fan of real crime shows and this is the first time I've ever been on the scene of a murder.'

'Well, you're in luck then. We don't get many murders at the hotel,' he said. 'The last one happened in 1929. A wealthy woman shot her gigolo through the heart. They hung her, you know.'

I didn't. It sounded a little like the Ruth Ellis case, and I wondered if he had made it up.

'The police haven't called it murder yet,' I said. 'It still might turn out to be an accident.'

He arched an eyebrow.

'An accident? It can't be an accident. I've only recently had those gargoyles recemented to fix them in place, for the insurance. If they were dislodged by mistake, the policy will be cancelled and we'll be screwed, so don't even suggest it.'

'What would happen then?'

'We'd have to close. It's unthinkable.'

'Can we go up to the balcony?' said Harry.

The manager glared at him.

'What for?'

'I'm a loss adjuster. I could check for you, if you like.'

'Well, now, that might be, yes, okay, it could be useful to know.'

He led us to the passageway where a dark stain still marked the floor and the metallic smell of oxidised blood lingered in the air. A shiver ran up my spine. I couldn't escape the feeling it could have been me lying there. My revulsion must have shown on my face because I saw Tim Boulting smirking at me. He paused at the bottom of the stairs and gestured dramatically at the balcony.

'You can see for yourself,' he said.

Harry and I climbed the steps to the balcony. It had been built out from the wall on a sturdy cantilevered structure. A guardrail ran along its length with spaces between the struts where the gargoyle flowerpots had been placed with their features facing out onto the passageway. I knelt down to examine one of them. Sure enough, it had been cemented to the balcony and did not budge when I tried to rock it. Whoever had done the job had added an extra piece of wood along the bottom of the guardrail to stop them falling off.

'This one seems pretty secure,' I said. 'Can you spot anything?'

'It's difficult to be sure. But the piece of wood at the bottom is hanging loose from the guardrail.'

'Not an accident then?'

'Maybe not. Although—'

'What?'

'Well, it seems unlikely anyone could have loosened the wooden rail, and freed the pot without someone at the wedding noticing. It would have taken at least five minutes to do it properly. Also, George had come up here to calm down. I'm surprised he didn't see or hear anything. How long did he spend up here before the pot fell?' said Harry, staggering to his feet.

'I'm not sure. We can ask him. That means anybody could have come up here before the wedding, and loosened the pot and the guardrail without anyone noticing.'

'Do you think they hid the tool up here?'

'Flo can tell us if the SOCOs found anything,' I said. 'She'll come by the Vintage if I offer her a cup cake.'

'Do you think we could search the men's changing room?'

'I already tried the door. It's locked. Maybe they haven't finished in there.'

We went back downstairs to find the manager waiting for us.

'Find anything?' he said.

'Nothing new, but we couldn't go into the changing room.'

'I've had them locked,' said Boulting.

'Can you open them for us?'

'Absolutely not. What do you think the chances are that the pot fell by accident?'

'It looks deliberate to me,' said Harry. 'You'll be fine with the insurance.'

'It's murder then?'

'I can't be sure. A woman died. Why do you care if its murder or not?'

The manager smirked.

'A murder will bring in new clients. We can do themed weekends with whodunits.'

My mouth fell open as I searched for a reply, but I couldn't think of a comeback. Harry put his arm around my shoulders and turned me towards the exit.

'We've got to go now,' he said. 'Thanks for the tour.'

'Next time I'll probably charge you.'

He didn't smile. Harry led me to the van despite my resistance. I chuntered under my breath as I got into the van.

'What a ghoul!' I said. 'He's planning on making money from Sharon's murder.'

'I gathered that. He'll do anything to keep the hotel open.'

'What if someone else wants to shut it?'

'What do you mean?' said Harry.

'Well, someone who knew about the insurance being vital. Could they have loosened the pot on purpose? Maybe they didn't mean to kill Sharon at all?'

'An accident? The problem with that is that we have a wedding full of suspects with motive to consider too.'

'I'm sure D.I. Antrim will be following their trails. Why don't we have a sniff around the hotel and find out who owns it and who might benefit if it failed?'

'That's got my vote.'

'Also, Mouse is champing at the bit to do something positive for his father. I'll get him to do an internet search and see what he finds.'

Harry started the van.

'Sounds good. We can stay out of Antrim's way and draw suspicion away from George at the same time,' he said.

'Let's get the food delivered to the Veterans' Hostel. Then we can go and have a cupcake in the Vintage. I'll ring Flo and see if she can pop by on her way home.'

Chapter 12

Mouse welcomed us to Second Home with hugs, but shook his head when I asked about sales. The only thing we were shifting was coffee and cake to the early Christmas shoppers. I thanked the late Mel Conrad once again for her great suggestion. We would not have survived without the Vintage. It reminded me that I could monetise the attic flat if I insulated the roof, a project I had on my list along with clearing the back garden. The list represented everything I had procrastinated on for the last year. I was glad to have another excuse to avoid all the tasks on it.

'Did you find out anything interesting?' said Mouse.

'I'll tell you all about it if you make a pot of tea. We've brought cupcakes from the wedding.'

'I'm not sure I want one of those.'

'That's okay. You don't have to eat one.'

After Mouse made the tea, Harry told him about the balcony and the despicable Tim Boulting.

'Murder weekends? Is he completely mad?'

'He's definitely peculiar, a bit like his doppelganger,' I said.

'And who's that?' said Harry.

'Do you remember the guy sitting beside me at the wedding dinner?'

'The odd looking one or the ancient one?'

'The weird guy. Didn't you recognise him?'

'I can't say I did.'

'He's Ray Colthard, the creepy guy who made a pass at me when I stripped off at the flea house.'

'Wait. What? Why didn't I hear about this,' said Mouse.

'Don't worry sweety. Nothing happened. But he could be the brother of the manager of the hotel, Tim Boulting. They're so alike.'

'We need to research the ownership of the hotel,' said Harry. 'If you want to help.'

'And the management by the sound of it,' said Mouse.

'If you can,' I said.

The door bell clanged as Flo Barrington, the forensic consultant, came into the shop. She puffed her way upstairs, lifting her heavy tweed skirt and resembling a Victorian farmer's wife with her rosy cheeks.

I made room for her on the banquette and served her tea and a cupcake. She shut her eyes in bliss as she bit into the cupcake.

'Oh my, these are heaven. Ghita's a genius. It's a pity so few people got to try them.'

Mouse pushed one with his finger. I could see he longed to try one, but I didn't say anything.

'Did the autopsy reveal any secrets?' I said.

'Nothing we didn't already know. The bride died from a blow to the head, likely caused by the gargoyle flower pot. We found white powder from the cement on the balcony and scattered on the floor of the passageway.'

'The manager of the hotel told us the flower pot had been recently secured for insurance. Did the SOCOs find any proof that it had been loosened?'

'I'm not sure. I'll check with them. D.I. Antrim is working on the theory that George killed Sharon in a crime of passion.'

'That would imply a spur of the moment decision, but he didn't have time to free the pot from the cement,' said Harry.

'Maybe George noticed the loose pot and saw his chance to get rid of Sharon in an accident?' said Flo. 'I don't believe that for a moment, mind you. George is hardly the passionate kind.'

'He had his moments,' I said. 'But this would be completely out of character.'

Mouse shuddered.

'Too much information,' he said, and grabbed a cupcake, groaning in ecstasy as the orange icing hit his tastebuds.

'Were there footprints in the dust?' I said.

'Yes, but the only clear ones belonged to George. He trampled any others with his large, PC Plod feet.'

'D.I. Antrim must be salivating if the only evidence points to George,' said Harry.

'He's in his element,' said Flo. 'I'm sorry I can't tell you more than that. This case is all about motive and opportunity. The means appears to be obvious.'

'Are the police treating it as murder?' said Mouse.

'They've classified it as an unexplained death. That will change if any clear evidence emerges.'

'What a mess,' I said. 'If I'd been a minute earlier, I might have saved her.'

'Or seen the killer,' said Harry.

'Are you sure you didn't? said Mouse.

'See the killer? I can't be certain. I suppose they could have come out of the passageway as I went in, but as soon as I saw the body on the ground my surroundings disappeared.'

'Did you smell anything?' said Flo.

'Blood, I remember that,' I said.

I closed my eyes and tried to visualise the scene, but the only thing I could see was the shape on the ground.

A faint scent of lavender drifted in and out of my memory, but I then remembered the diffuser in the women's toilet. I could recall George's shocked expression. The way the blood had drained out of his face in an instance when he noticed the body.

'He thought it was me,' I said.

'D.I. Antrim?' said Flo.

'No. George. He thought Sharon was me and vice versa. He asked me what was going on down there, in the passageway. When he saw the body, he asked me if Tanya had been hurt. We were wearing the same green, velvet trouser suit.'

'And you have the same hair,' said Harry. 'You could have been sisters.'

'Why were you wearing the same suit?' said Mouse.

'A horrible coincidence,' I said. 'She changed into it for leaving the wedding. That's why I went to see her. She said she had a surprise for me. I thought she had a gift or something, but maybe she wanted us to have a laugh about wearing the same clothes.'

'How long had she been wearing the suit?' said Flo.

'She'd only just changed, because she was still wearing her wedding dress five minutes before then when she asked me to come to the women's changing room for a surprise.'

'That means no one except for you saw her wearing the trouser suit,' said Mouse.

'No one except the killer,' said Harry.

'Doesn't that mean it could have been a mistake?' said Flo.

'Got it in one,' I said. 'I may have been the target and not Sharon.'

'Does that mean you still are?' said Mouse. 'If they killed the wrong person, they may still want to murder you. You could be in danger.'

'He's right,' said Flo. 'There may be someone out there with a grudge.'

'But who on earth would try to kill me? What possible reason would they have?' I said.

'Seriously, you need to be careful,' said Mouse. 'I'll do some research on the hotel and Sharon's family. Maybe we can find out who had a motive to kill you.'

'I'd like to see them get past me,' said Harry, puffing out his chest, and I beamed at him.

But the theory held water. I had an uneasy feeling they were right.

'I heard Theresa and Fintan talking outside the church. They were discussing how Sharon had intended to swindle George,' I said. 'I'm pretty sure Fintan saw me listening. He made a throat slitting gesture at me from the top table.'

'I knew that family were poison. Fintan has a record as long as your arm. Did you tell D.I. Antrim about Fintan and Theresa?' said Flo.

'Yes, I told him everything I could remember from the day.'

'I'll check the forensics again. The SOCO team collected fingerprints from the guardrails and door handle of the men's changing room,' said Flo.

'Did they check the women's changing room too?' said Harry.

'I don't know. But both changing rooms are still locked. I'll check with the team,' said Flo. 'Don't go wandering about in the dark by yourself until we find out what's going on.'

'I won't,' I said, lying.

'She won't,' said Harry, with more conviction.

'I'll lock her in to the Grotty Hovel,' said Mouse. 'Hades can guard the door.'

Chapter 13

Harry and Mouse wrapped me in cotton wool after that. I actually enjoyed being molly coddled for a few days, but soon I began to feel claustrophobic. Helen had her hands full with George, who had entered a period of deep mourning and remorse. She fed him three times a day, but he hardly ate any of it. He never spoke except to say please and thank you, and he struggled to shower or get dressed. Helen found this extremely distressing, but she soldiered on, offering support with her solid presence and kindness. Harry went round to see George 'to cheer him up a bit' and came back gloomy and shocked.

'He's in bad shape,' he told me. 'I think he's suffering from PTSD. It's a good thing Helen doesn't have any booze in the house.'

'Should he see a shrink?' I said. 'I know it helped me through the worst days.'

'Not yet. He's not in a receptive mood. He blames himself for Sharon's death, but he won't discuss her duplicity. Give him time. He'll come round.'

Grace extracted the interest on her pound of flesh for holding the fort at Second Home by getting Harry to do some deliveries for her, but I didn't mind. Harry's agitation surrounding the circumstances of the murder made him over-protective of me. I felt like a gated schoolgirl, dying to sneak out without anyone noticing. Hades took an avid interest in my constant presence in the house. He lurked close by when I tried to research the Walsh and Hurley families. I found the remains of several mice laid out by the fridge door in case I got hungry. He even deigned to share the sofa with me while I curled up with Antiques Roadshow and Lovejoy on repeat. Sometimes, he sat just out of reach, but I pretended not to notice. Olivia had told me to ignore him if I wanted him to cave in, and she studied behavioural therapy.

The novelty of being at home soon wore off. There is only so much cleaning and organising you can do before you run out of things to do. The constant sleet and rain did not encourage me to venture outside and cut back the brambles, so the back garden glowered at me through the gloom of the shortening days. I needed the hacking skills of Mouse to find information in the hidden corners of the internet, but he spent all day in the shop, sometimes with Roz, who had recently been at sea with Ed on his small trawler. They were developing a new clientele for their high-end catch of lobsters. They also worked with the council policing the marine reserve in Seacastle Bay and diving the kelp forests to survey juvenile fish populations. In a way, David Foster's death had been the best thing to ever happen to them. It had put a bomb under their marriage and revived their passion for life and for each other. Roz blossomed and Ed grew less grumpy as they took advantage of their new opportunities to buy the cottage where they lived.

I could tell by the way he burst in and went straight to the table to open his laptop that Mouse had discovered something interesting. He tapped the keys, his brow furrowed and his tongue poking out between his lips.

'Ta dah!' he said, swinging the laptop around so I could see it too.

I pulled up a chair and gazed at the screen. Tarton Manor House had belonged to the Sheldon family since a certain Thomas Sheldon had built it in the 1820s with the profits of their textile business which exploded during the industrial revolution. The family had lost much of their fortune in the twentieth century due to ill-judged investments in mining shares like Poseidon Nickel. The sole heir to Tarton Manor House, Lydia Sheldon, had caved in to the inevitable and sold the house to developers in the 1990s. She had disappeared off the radar for more than twenty years, but Mouse had traced her to a council house on an estate west of the Seacastle railway station.

'How the mighty are fallen,' I said. 'I can't imagine she took it well, being turfed out of the family home and losing everything.'

'Do you think it's worth talking to her?'

'Definitely. If Harry will let me out of the house.'

'I'll go with you tomorrow morning. Roz can run the café for an hour or two. She's a dab hand with the coffee machine, and the Christmas rush has not started yet.'

'What if Lydia Sheldon works during the day?'

'Then we'll have to find her at work. Harry would kill me if we went at night.'

'I suppose he has a point. We ought to be careful until we know discover who was the intended victim. Did you find anything else?'

'I did a search on the company who developed the hotel. They appear to be a bunch of cowboy builders. The present owners bought the house from Lydia Sheldon, the last of the line, in its original state and paid for the redevelopment.'

'Excellent. This may be a dead end, but there's only one way of finding out.'

Lydia Sheldon lived in Prince Albert Close, a neat estate off the main road to Lancing. The houses were typical 1960s build, with gabled roofs and porches at the front entrance. Most people had filled their porches with plants and bicycles and wellington boots. Outside, box hedges and bare rose bushes stood firm against the encroaching winter. Sparrows squabbled in the bushes and a tabby cat slunk along the pavement looking for trouble or avoiding the local dogs, I couldn't tell which. Lydia's house sat on a turning circle so it had a truncated frontage and a more expansive rear garden. The pebble dash exterior had turned grey with age, but the flower beds and path were weed-free. Mouse lifted the large door knocker which looked as if it might have come from a grander door. When it fell, it echoed down the hallway and soon a tall, slim woman in a pale pink twinset and pearls glided to the door. She opened it halfway and peered out.

'Can I help you,' she said.

I'm so sorry to bother you. I know it's an inconvenience, but I hope you may be able to help us,' said Mouse, with his best handsome prince smile.

The look on her face suggested she believed us to be Jehovah's Witnesses or Mormons come to bore her rigid or extract money from her. She had no intention of helping us and seemed about to say so. I stepped forward with my most ingratiating smile.

'I'm an investigative reporter doing research on the loss of important country houses to development. I'm looking for cases of injustice and possible fraud that I can follow up and expose. Tarton Manor House came up as a possible victim of fraud in my research. My assistant, Andrew looked you up and we decided to come and see you.'

I emphasised the words important and injustice, and I watched as a fanatical gleam lit up her eyes. As I had anticipated, she did not ask how we had found her; she just wanted an audience for her grievance.

'I might be able to spare you half an hour,' she said. 'I'm terribly busy you know.'

We followed her down the spotless hallway into an equally clean sitting room. A cup of tea and some chocolate biscuits on a plate sat on a small table beside a recliner. Countdown showed on the TV screen, paused for her to answer the door. I resisted the temptation to draw attention to it. Everyone's definition of busy is different. She did not offer us anything to drink. We sat on a chintz couch opposite the fire place and Mouse took out his iPad. Lydia Sheldon returned the recliner to an upright position and sat down, her back rigid with her legs just above the ground.

'Ask your questions,' she said.

'When did you sell Tarton Manor House?' said Mouse.

'1993'

'Can you tell me how much you received for it?' I said.

'No. It's none of your business.'

'Um. Okay. Did you receive a fair price for the house? I mean in comparison to the market value.'

'I know what you meant. Absolutely not. The Tippings swindled me. They forced me to sell at far less than the asking price.'

'Forced you? How so?'

'Extortion,' she said.

'Why didn't you go to the police,' I said.

She narrowed her eyes.

'As if they'd have done anything. The police were in cahoots with the Tippings. Money talks.'

'You've lost me,' I said. 'If I'm going to help, you need to explain exactly what happened?'

'The Tippings are a wealthy Brighton family, a husband-and-wife team, Gary and Delia. He used to work with a big developer in London and set out on his own in the 90s.'

Mouse tapped away on his iPad, head down, tongue tip out.

'How did you meet them?'

'They turned up at the manor house. I hadn't even put it up for sale yet.'

She pulled at a stray thread in her skirt and then stopped when a seam began to unravel. I waited. Mouse glanced at me, but I shook my head. The room did not offer many distractions. A rather lovely landscape hung over the gas fireplace, featuring Tarton Manor House. A large oak grew in the place where the conservatory now stood. I suspected the painting had survived the contents sale of Tarton Manor. Hereford cattle ruminated under the oak while storm clouds gathered in the background. It couldn't have been more apt. A pair of silver candlesticks sat at either end of the mantlepiece. Wax had dripped down their stems and into the silver trays below them. Everything in its place. Finally, she sniffed.

'They told me they had information about the state of my finances which they would pass on to the bank holding my mortgage. My husband had practically bankrupted us with his profligate spending and then he had died of a heart attack in the arms of his paramour. He had a life insurance policy with Safe Haven, which could have saved the house, but they kept stalling until I had been backed into a corner. I had managed to stave off disaster by moving money around, but I had come to the end of the line. The Tippings offered me enough to clear the debts and buy myself this palace.'

She flung her arms out.

'Why wouldn't Safe Haven pay out?'

'The Tippings had a mole who pretended to be investigating my husband's death. Every time we got close to a payout, he or she would invent some other reason to stop the payment. I would never have been in the situation in the first place if it weren't for my husband's cavalier attitude.'

'And then they developed it into a hotel. You must have been resentful.'

'There's no past tense involved. I'm still as angry as I ever was. I'll never stop trying to get it back.'

'By fair means or foul?' said Mouse.

'The end justifies the means,' she said. 'A little bird told me they're in a little trouble themselves with the insurance.'

My blood ran cold at this nonchalant comment. Could this be revenge? But why kill Sharon?

'A woman died there on Saturday, you know,' I said. 'Her wedding day as it happens.'

'I heard about that. An unfortunate accident,' she said, smirking. 'Or karma? Who knows?'

'Do you?' I said.

She stood up.

'I don't like your tone,' she said. 'Or the direction the conversation is taking. The Tippings swindled me and took my house. That's the only relevant information you need for your report. The rest is coincidence and hearsay. Now get out of my house.'

Chapter 14

Our visit to Lydia Sheldon had thrown up a new lead, but not one which gave me any clarity. Her mission to get back Tarton Manor House did not seem to have anything to do with either Sharon or me. I struggled to see the connection with Sharon's death. Lydia's reference to insurance problems had awoken my curiosity though. What sort of problems? If the flower pot had fallen down due to negligence they might lose their insurance, but surely they could find another company to insure the hotel? I asked Mouse to research reasons an insurance company wouldn't insure a property, while I made a list of possible suspects and motives.

I couldn't discount Lydia Sheldon. She appeared quite ruthless and I didn't need further explanation of her motive. George had to figure in the list, whether I could believe it of him or not. The possibility he shoved the flower pot off in a fit of pique and killed Sharon by mistake had to be considered. His furious expression as he sat at the top table had ingrained itself in my memory. I couldn't recall ever seeing him so livid. Did he lose his temper for an instant? I couldn't interrogate him about it. D.I. Antrim would have to do that. I remained convinced of George's innocence, but I was hardly a neutral observer.

And then there were the Hurleys, Fintan and Theresa. Even Sharon had barely tolerated their brand of pushy capitalism. Fintan had a record as long as his arm and Theresa was hiding a world of secrets behind the China doll makeup. I found it hard to believe Theresa would kill her sister, even by mistake, but I had plenty of excuses to talk to her. Fintan would be more difficult. Harry might have an idea on that score. He would definitely have to come with me for any cosy chat I arranged. Fintan had a history of violence and plenty of reasons for knocking off his sister-in-law, all of them emblazoned with pictures of the Queen.

Mouse brought me a cup of tea. He had a cheeky grin on his face.

'What did you find out?' I said.

'We need to ask some questions about the state of the hotel buildings,' he said.

'Does that affect the insurance premiums?'

'It depends. If the hotel has had any subsidence, it will be almost impossible for them to change insurers. The original insurers can't back out unless they have a genuine excuse which doesn't involve subsidence.'

'Like negligence? A loose pot killing a guest seems to qualify.'

'But the gargoyle had been deliberately levered out of its fitting. I'm not sure if that counts,' he said.

'The crux of this matter seems to revolve around the pot then. Rather than a cold-blooded calculation, the loosened pot seems to indicate an accident or unpremeditated murder.'

'We need to talk to the insurance company.'

'Some insider information would be useful. Do you fancy some part time work in the hotel gardens? I'm sure Roz told me she had a cousin who worked at the hotel.'

'She did. I'll text her and see if she can swing it.'

'Why don't we go and see her? I'll be perfectly safe with the two of you in the shop with me. Just don't tell Harry.'

'You can't stay inside for ever. Anyway, Fintan is in the police cells after going on a bender since the murder and trying to beat up P.C. Brennan.'

'I'm not going to ask you how you know that. Do you think he killed Sharon? Maybe he's drinking out of guilt?'

'Or grief?'

We drove to Second Home in the Mini and were lucky to get a parking space in a side road nearby. Mouse insisted on getting out first and scanning the roads for danger. The only sign of that were two seagulls having a bad-tempered tug of war over a chicken bone one of them had found in a discarded Kentucky Fried Chicken takeaway box. We still trotted to the shop to be on the safe side. Roz's face lit up as we entered and she jumped off the stool behind the counter to greet us.

'How are you holding up,' she said. 'What an appalling tragedy. I heard all about it.'

'What are people saying?' I said.

'Most are calling it a tragic accident,' she said. 'But my cousin Dermot isn't so sure.'

'Is he the gardener at Tarton Manor House?' said Mouse.

'Yes, that's him.'

'Do you think I could get some part time work at the hotel to do some digging?'

'Is that metaphorical or physical?' said Roz.

'Both, I s'pose.'

'I don't know. The winter garden needs very little maintenance, but he'd come and speak to you here if you offered him coffee and cake. Shall I give him a call?'

'That would be wonderful. If he can manage it.'

'It's dark after five. I'll ask him to come when he finishes his shift.'

While Roz called her cousin, I busied myself at the back of the shop emptying boxes from house clearances

Harry and I had done. I found one containing the beautiful milk glass we had salvaged from a nicotine stained flat in one of the tower blocks along the eastern shore of Seacastle. We had already cleaned and rewired two gorgeous lamps, a Murano flower light and an Odeon clamshell, which Grace had snapped up immediately. This box yielded a vintage Fostoria Winburn aqua blue milk glass creamer, a Westmoreland milk glass sawtooth pattern butter dish, a Fenton Art glass periwinkle hobnail jar, and a ruffled ginger jar vase. The stench of old ashtray almost knocked me out as I unwrapped them and placed them in a bucket of hot water mixed with spirit vinegar. I gently rubbed them to remove the brown nicotine film and used a toothbrush to clean the tight spots. Years of stains came away and revealed the milk glass underneath, protected from wear and tear by their status as ornaments. These pieces were never used, only gazed upon by covetous eyes, so they were in mint condition.

Roz's cousin Dermot came in at half past five on the dot. He had obviously made an effort to wash his hands and damp down his crown of grey curls with water, but they sprang up every time he moved his head. He seemed nervous of touching anything, but when he spotted a fine farmer's chair, he ran his hand along the arm rest with gentle reverence.

'My father had one of these,' he said. 'I bet he never thought he'd see it in a shop for sale again. I like the idea of vintage. Everything is recycled eventually, even ourselves.'

He gave Roz an embarrassed hug and shook our hands, before sitting carefully down on one of our kitchen chairs. He accepted a cup of tea and a flapjack which he ate in three bites. I offered him a second, but he shook his head. I could see he wanted it, but I didn't want to make him uneasy.

'Roz tells me you were up at the Manor on Saturday,' he said.

'That's right. My ex-husband got married again and I organised the wedding.'

'Couldn't wait to get rid of him, eh? Strange how his bride didn't survive the night. That's karma for you.'

He took a slurp of his tea and grinned at me, waiting. I did not take the bait.

'Have you worked at Tarton Manor House for long?' I said.

'Since I were a lad.'

'Did you work for Lydia Sheldon?' said Mouse.

'And her father. I'm close to retiring now. Just need another year of stamps.'

'It must have been a big change when the Tippings took over.'

'A shock. First, they got rid of me, but they called me back once the redevelopment had finished. No one else knows the house like I do.'

'And now? Are you in charge of general maintenance or only gardening.'

'Mostly gardening, but they are understaffed so I often have to pitch in and help with other stuff.'

'I guess there must be constant problems with the age of the buildings.'

His relaxed demeanour changed.

'Are you asking me about the flower pot? I told them not to use those on the balcony. It's nothing to do with me.'

He stood up to leave, but Roz put her hand on his arm.

'Calm down. They're not accusing you of anything. They need your help.'

'Doesn't sound like it.'

'I'm sorry,' I said. 'I'm interested in the state of the buildings because I spoke to Lydia Sheldon and she insinuated the hotel would have insurance problems in the near future. Do you know anything about that?'

He shifted in his seat.

'Nothing I'm prepared to talk about right now. The Sheldons always treated me correctly.'

'That's fair enough,' said Mouse. 'Actually, I wondered if I could help you out in the gardens sometime.'

Dermot laughed.

'And what would a modern young man like you be doing in the dirt?'

'The back garden of our house is completely overgrown and we want to plant some rose bushes. I thought I might learn something from you, if that's okay.'

'I'm laying in the mulch tomorrow if you fancy it.'

I could see from Mouse's face he hadn't the first idea what that meant, but he nodded.

'Great. That would be fantastic. What time would you like me to be there?'

'First light. About eight o'clock.'

Mouse looked at me.

'No problem. I'll drive you over,' I said.

Chapter 15

The next morning, we were up bright and early to deliver Mouse to Dermot's care at Tarton Manor House. I could see him looking forlorn and uncertain in my rearview mirror, but I didn't repent. He might pick up some crucial information about the hotel during a day of mulching. Then my phone rang and I pulled in to the side of the road to answer it. D.I. Antrim had summoned me to the station for a formal interview. I had been so wrapped up in our sleuthing I had completely forgotten he was investigating the case in an official capacity. No doubt George would be next in line if he hadn't already been questioned. I tried to organise my thoughts and visualise the evening in detail. I had made copious notes which I intended to pass on to him.

Nerves fluttered in my stomach as I drove to the police station like winter butterflies awakened by a warm day in winter. I had a feeling D.I. Antrim would use my evidence to corner George and try to force him to confess. No matter how many times I told myself George couldn't have done it, I couldn't escape the fact he had motive, means and opportunity. George himself had drilled me on the mantra of there being no such thing as coincidence in a murder investigation. Refusing to dismiss anything as a coincidence had helped me greatly in my former career on *Uncovering the Truth*. Mind you, as a group we seemed to be attracting more than our fair share of murders in Seacastle. Roz's joke about me being the new Jessica Fletcher hit close to home.

Carol Burns loomed like the ghost of Christmas past behind the reception desk of the police station. I had a strong feeling of déjà vu as her cheap perfume swamped my senses. Memories surfaced of my early days with George when I used to pop in with his forgotten lunch-box as an excuse to see him. She had a habit of spraying herself from head to foot with Charlie to disguise the smell of drink that followed her around. She couldn't hide her smug expression when I entered. I felt like slapping her to wipe it off her face.

'Fancy seeing you here,' I said.

'Sally is on holiday, so D.I. Antrim asked me if I'd cover for her.'

'I thought I had entered a scene from *Back to the Future.*'

'He needed experience behind the desk at this difficult time.'

'Can I go through?'

'D.I. Antrim is busy with another suspect.'

'I'm a suspect? How exciting!' I said. 'I thought I'd only be helping the police with their inquiries.'

'Weren't you the last person to see the victim alive?'

'In a manner of speaking. She died in my arms.'

Carol sneered at this exaggeration.

'She got what was coming to her if you ask me. George is far too good for a woman like that.'

'Like what?'

'A jumped-up chav. Look at her family. The apple doesn't fall far from the tree. I don't know why he didn't go for someone more suitable.'

She straightened the lizard pin on her jacket and stuck out her ample chest. I realised with a start she meant herself. I stifled a snort. George did not approve of Carol Burns. He had found her drinking unprofessional and he had been instrumental in hastening her retirement. It must have irritated her beyond measure when he set up house with her replacement, Sharon. I felt tempted to tell her George had moved in with my sister but I didn't want to be unkind either. Also, I had no idea if Helen's nascent feelings had survived his presence or if George reciprocated any of them.

Before I could sit down, P.C. Brennan popped his head around the door.

'He's ready for you.'

'Thanks, Joe.'

I followed him through the safety door and into the main working part of the station. I received some cheery waves from George's crew. I can't imagine what they made of my interview so soon after my involvement with the murder at the Pavilion Theatre. I waved back as if being a suspect in a murder case were the most normal thing in the world.

D.I. Antrim had already entered the interview room and sat down. He had crossed his long legs and he resembled some species of black cricket, all limbs and skinny torso.

'We meet again,' he said. 'Are you ready to get started?'

I nodded and removed my shoes to avoid the inevitable electric shocks from the static. Then I folded myself into a plastic chair, mirroring him exactly. A tiny smirk appeared on his face, but he didn't say anything. Instead, he switched on the recording device and recited his name and the date, and named me as the interviewee. He took a piece of wrinkled paper from his hip pocket, which appeared to have been salvaged from a wastepaper basket, and he smoothed it out on the table top.

'If you don't mind, I'd like to start at the beginning,' he said. 'How did you meet George?'

I smiled, despite my discomfort.

'The first time?' I said.

'I'm in the mood for romance,' he said, and I had a glimpse of the real person behind the police façade in his shy grin.

'My car suffered a flat tyre on the road to Shoreham, so I pulled into the lay-by to change it. When I took my jack out of the boot, I realised a piece had gone missing or been left behind somewhere, so I couldn't remove the tyre. I didn't carry a cell phone at the time. I'm a bit of a Luddite, or I was, until Mouse invaded my life. It got dark and I waited, stranded in the lay-by. Just then a car pulled in and George got out. He had intended on relieving himself in the bushes, but when he saw me, his plans changed.'

'That is romantic.'

'The rest is history. Ancient history now.'

'Why did you break up?'

'Sharon came along at a difficult time in our marriage. I had a bad bout of clinical depression, due to exhaustion, I think. Anyway, I had to give up my job and became withdrawn. George couldn't cope with the change. He's a little old fashioned when it comes to mental illness. Sharon reminded him of the real me and she made it clear she liked him too. I had no idea they were having an affair until George asked me for a divorce. I'm supposed to be an investigative reporter, but I didn't notice I'd lost my husband to another woman.'

I smiled ruefully.

'Did you hate him?'

'Hate George? Absolutely not. He gave me the best thing I've ever had.'

'Mouse?'

'Yes. I love Mouse more than I ever loved George to tell you the truth. George and I were always very different and I made the mistake of compromising myself into a corner for him.'

'Do you have a boyfriend?'

'Yes, not that it's any of your business.'

'Is he jealous of George?'

'Sometimes. George couldn't draw a line under our marriage, and recently he turned up to my house when Harry and I were together. I think Harry tolerated me organising George's marriage, because it would give us a chance to get along without him popping in constantly. And, weirdly, Harry and George get on like a house on fire.'

'I heard George is staying with your sister, Helen. Isn't that even weirder?'

'We decided he couldn't stay with me in case you thought we were in cahoots over Sharon. His house is still out of bounds. He had to stay somewhere, and we are his only family now.'

D.I. Antrim sighed.

'Honestly, I'd arrest you all for incest if I could. I've never known such a convoluted situation.'

'It's tied together by affection, not hate. Sharon told George she was having his baby and we wanted to be involved because it would have been Mouse's brother.'

'But there was no baby. Did George know that?'

'Sharon told him she lost it, soon after the ceremony. But I heard her tell Theresa she had never been pregnant.'

'Why pretend?'

'She intended on taking him to the cleaners. Her sister and brother-in-law were complicit in the scam.'

'That must have been shocking for you to hear. Were you angry with her?'

'I don't remember. She lurched over to me shortly afterwards, and told me to come and see her at the changing rooms. She said she had a surprise for me.'

'Did she give you something?'

'No. I think she wanted to show me her going away outfit. We had exactly the same suit on.'

'And nothing else?'

'Absolutely nothing. I was a little surprised. I thought she had bought me something for organising the wedding.'

'Did she tell you what happened to her?'

'No, she just said 'surprise' and died.'

'Did you see anyone else in the passageway?'

'No. I've gone over the scene many times in my mind. I saw Tim Boulting the hotel manager there earlier, but I can't recall seeing him then. The only new thing I can remember is the swinging door to the main hotel squeaking. I think someone may have used it to leave, but I can't be sure.'

'That's convenient.'

I glared at him.

'Do you really imagine any of this is convenient? One minute we were celebrating a wedding and the imminent arrival of a new baby, and the next we had a dead bride, a grieving husband and a web of lies to sort out.'

'Fair enough. Is there anything else you can tell me about the day or about Sharon that might help us?'

'You might want to look closely at her siblings. I'm not sure either of them has any scruples when it comes to getting what they want. Of course, the flower pot is the key to all this. Who pushed it off the balcony and did they intend to kill Sharon with it, or anyone at all for that matter?'

'Or you.'

'Or me.'

'I presume you're interfering with my investigation as usual. I'd appreciate it if you'd inform me of any firm leads you get to prevent duplication of effort.'

'And will you tell me about yours?'

'Oh, I'm sure Flo will tell you most things, just keep police information to yourself and I won't arrest you yet.'

I didn't bother denying it.

Chapter 16

I collected Mouse from Tarton Manor House at sundown about five o'clock in the afternoon. The Georgian house looked spectacular under the orange skies which reflected off the roof of the conservatory and make it look like a Terry's Chocolate Orange. Flocks of crows swept over the roof and roosted in the trees nearby. I hardly recognised the filthy, weary boy with mud-stained clothes who waited for me with Dermot on the steps of the conservatory. Dermot gave me a cheery wave as I drove up to them, and slapped Mouse on the back. They shook hands and Mouse came over to the car. I could tell from his barely suppressed air of excitement he had extracted some important information from Dermot. He plopped onto the passenger seat of the Mini and showed me his blisters.

'War wounds,' he said. 'And worth every one to winkle the truth out of a man determined not to reveal it.'

'Harry's coming over with fish and chips,' I said. 'If you can bear to hold it in until then?'

'I hope he's coming early.'

'Text him. He's doing a delivery for the Wongs today. He shouldn't be delayed.'

I was about to drive off when something occurred to me. I wound down the window and beckoned to Dermot.

'Do you want a lift anywhere?' I said.

He beamed at me, but wiped his hands on his trousers and shook his head.

'I'm a right mess,' he said. 'I wouldn't like to make your car dirty.'

'And Mouse isn't? Hop in and give me directions. We'll have you home in a jiffy.'

Dermot got into the back and put on his seatbelt. We set out towards Seacastle and, halfway there, Dermot directed me down a side road with neat bungalows either side. We stopped outside one with clipped box hedges around a pristine lawn. Dermot beckoned me out of the car so he could speak to me alone.

'There's not many people left who have proper manners,' he said. 'I told young Mouse to watch out for the Hurleys. That Fintan Hurley is trouble. But there's something I didn't tell Mouse, because, well, it's about his father.'

'George? What's he done now?'

'Oh, I ain't saying he done nothing, but he turned up at the big house a couple of days before the wedding and wandered around the conservatory. He stayed in there about half an hour and then he left again. I wouldn't have told you, only Mouse said something about the flower pot being loosened on the balcony before the wedding. And you doing an investigation and all. Course, the Hurleys were there on their own too, so there's loads of choice if you think one of them done it on purpose.'

My blood turned cold at this revelation, but I tried not to appear shocked. I nodded sagely.

'There certainly is. Thanks for telling me. Can you keep an eye out for a discarded chisel in the garden? It's a long shot, but someone may have got rid of it in a bin or something. I'll find out what George was doing there as soon as I can.'

'I'll text Roz if I find anything. Thanks for the lift. The lad's a bit soft, but I can use him again if he's willing.'

'I'll let him know. Thanks.'

I got back into the car and avoided Mouse's questioning glance. This new piece of information had thrown me. What on earth was George doing at the conservatory before the wedding? He's shown no interest in being involved with the preparations. I would have to ask him. It never occurred to me he might lie.

When we got home, I sent Mouse upstairs to shower and put cream on his blisters, while I laid the table and turned on the oven. Then I sat on the sofa puzzling over the myriad of possible suspects and motives. I had never expected to be seriously considering George as one of them, but he had motive, and now it seemed opportunity too. I couldn't discount him. I texted him and asked if he had time for a chat. When he did not answer me straight away, I suspected Helen had a moratorium on phones at the dinner table. He'd answer when he could.

So far, I hadn't had time to consider the role of Fintan and Theresa in the tragedy. Sharon herself had told me they would have been quite happy to eject her from her own business, but I couldn't believe they'd go that far. Their screams of horror when they saw her body had seemed genuine enough, but a five-minute gap between the last time I spoke to her and finding her body gave plenty of time for either of them to have run up the stairs, pushed the flower pot off the balcony and slipped back to the table without being noticed. There was also the possibility they had gone out through the main lobby of the hotel and doubled back into the doors of the conservatory. Since everyone used that entrance to come and go and for smoke breaks, it would have been simple to mingle with the other wedding guests.

As I fretted over my notes, I heard a key in the door and Harry came in carrying a takeaway bag loaded with battered cod and chips. I gave him a big hug and breathed in his odour of soap and toast mixed with a tang of salt and vinegar from the soggy packages. He glanced at the pile of notes scattered on the sofa.

'Making any progress?' he said.

'More suspects and an absence of clues, but Mouse spent the day with Dermot, Roz's cousin, in the gardens of Tarton Manor House, so he's dying to tell us all about it.'

'Get the food in the oven then, and I'll pour us a glass of wine. Does Mouse want cider?'

'I expect so, gardening is thirsty work.'

'It certainly is,' said Mouse, coming down the stairs. 'Those fish and chips smell amazing.'

'I'm putting them in the oven to crisp up a bit. Why don't you tell us what Dermot told you?'

We all sat on the sofa and sipped our drinks. Hades snuggled up to Harry and purred loudly to annoy me. Mouse cleared his throat.

'Do you remember the painting in Lydia Sheldon's house,' he asked me.

'The one over the fireplace?'

'That's the one. I don't know if you noticed, but the artist had painted a large oak tree on the righthand side of it.'

I shut my eyes and tried to visualise it. Sure enough, I could recall its slightly primitive style, but also its unmistakeable shape.

'Where the conservatory is now?'

Exactly.'

'You've lost me,' said Harry. 'What's that got to do with anything?'

'The Tippings cut down the oak when they bought the house,' said Mouse. 'Dermot told me the oak had been planted when the Sheldon family built the house. The tree was synonymous with Tarton Manor, but that didn't save it when the Tippings bought it. They blamed the oak for subsidence in the main house despite protests by the Sheldons. The insurance company sided with the Tippings, and they let them cut it down. Shortly afterwards, the Tippings got planning permission for the conservatory. Dermot says the whole thing seemed dodgy to him.'

'But it has backfired on them now,' I said.

'What do you mean?' said Harry.

'Once you report subsidence to an insurance company they are obliged to pay for the damage, but no other company will take on the property afterwards. The insurance company is trapped in the deal unless they can manufacture a pretext for refusing to insure Tarton Manor House. Lydia Sheldon knew that. In my opinion, she's perfectly capable of giving them the excuse they needed,' I said.

'With no insurance, the hotel would be worthless. Lydia could buy it back for almost nothing,' said Mouse.

'But why would Lydia Sheldon want a house she can't insure?' said Harry.

'What if she has information about the tree scam?' said Mouse. 'She could reverse the decision by bringing the evidence to the insurance company.'

'That supposes the original mole has left,' I said. 'Oh no!'

'What?' said Mouse.

'Save the chips! They'll burn.'

Chapter 17

George turned up at the Vintage the next day. His haggard face and loose clothing told me even Helen's home cooking had not prevented him from losing weight due to stress. He did not yell out a greeting, as he often did, but crept up the stairs like someone arriving late from a pub crawl. I couldn't believe how much Sharon's death had defeated and diminished him.

'I blame myself, Tan,' he said, avoiding my eyes. 'If I'd left her earlier, and refused to get married, she might still be alive.'

'You can't believe that.'

'I do. I killed her, as sure as if I pushed the flower pot off the balcony by myself.'

'And did you?'

His eyeballs almost popped out of his head.

'How can you ask me that? No, I couldn't.'

'Not even after she told you about the baby?'

'I had calmed down by the time it happened. I realised I could divorce her without fuss and not feel guilty in the slightest.'

I stared at him, trying to read his mind, but he seemed oblivious to my unease. As usual, he only thought about how things had affected him. Nobody else mattered. This annoyed me sufficiently to rile me a little and give me courage to ask him the question that hovered in my head.

'I spoke to the gardener at Tarton Manor Hall, and he tells me you visited the conservatory alone before the wedding. You wouldn't come and see it when I asked. Why did you go there without me?'

'What are you insinuating?'

'I'm not insinuating anything. I'm asking you what you were doing at the conservatory. The flowerpot had recently been cemented into place. It couldn't have fallen unless somebody had loosened it before the wedding.'

'Somebody? You mean me?'

'I'm not accusing you of anything. I'm asking you what you were doing there.'

George stood up and pushed his chair back.

'I don't have to tell you. You're not a detective. I don't know why I came.'

'You don't have to tell me, but remember, D.I. Antrim may find out about your visit.'

'Are you threatening me?'

'That's the reality. I thought you'd prefer to tell me rather than him, that's all.'

'You thought wrong.'

He rushed down the stairs, tripping and almost falling in his hurry to leave, swinging wildly from the banister before stabilising himself. I felt shellshocked by his sudden departure. What on earth had been so private that he couldn't tell me? George could not keep a secret. His boastful nature made him prone to gaffs and blurting out private information. There was a reason D.I. Antrim felt superior. George had done well in his job because he had me to guide him and tamp down his tendency to reveal details of his investigations to untrustworthy audiences. Once we had divorced, his weaknesses became glaringly obvious, and had increased the danger of him being encouraged to retire early. Only the dearth in qualified officers kept him in his job. He needed guidance, but his superintendent had the sensitivity of a warthog and had no tools to recognise or help George to be a better officer.

I tried to busy myself decorating the shop for Christmas, but I felt unsettled by George's weird reaction. The shop ledger didn't improve my mood. The numbers jumped and skipped around the pages making me dizzy. I could see we were in trouble, but not how much. George owed me for the wedding and I didn't know how to ask him for the money after all that had happened. I couldn't pay for it myself, nor had I considered that as an option, but if he didn't come up with the money, Second Home would go under.

The sun came out from behind the grey blur that substituted for the sky during the early winter, and lit up the pavements with its slanted rays. The temptation to escape the shop became too strong. There were two slices of orange drizzle cake left in the cabinet upstairs in the Vintage café. I wrapped them in a napkin which I placed in a Ziploc bag. Then, I hung the closed sign on the door and stuck a post-it-note underneath, which read 'back soon'. I avoided a time slot in case I couldn't face returning. Outside, the street almost echoed with emptiness. Only the raucous gulls on the rooftops broke the silence. The town felt as dead as Sharon Walsh, despite the Christmas decorations in the shop windows. Some man-sized, wooden nutcracker dolls had been lashed to the lampposts at intervals along the street. Their rictus expressions gave them an evil rather than festive air.

My thick down coat kept out the worst of the wind which blew me along the street to Grace and Max Wong's shop. Their window stood out with its elaborate wreaths, and baubles made from gamebird feathers. I gazed in at the expensive presents Grace had placed there to tempt desperate husbands and wives. She really had exquisite taste. Suddenly, her disembodied white face appeared from behind a bookcase. I almost screamed until I realised that she had poked it through a heavy velvet curtain at the back of the display. She winked at me as she reached for an ornate pistol lying on a three-legged table near the front. I waved and pushed my way into the shop where she had placed the pistol into an original box with its twin brother. Then she wrapped it in embossed paper under the critical gaze of the buyer, a woman in a mink coat which screamed real at me.

'I'll be with you in a minute,' said Grace.

While she dealt with her client, I had a good nose around the shop. I recognised several pieces from my former stock. She could sell them for far greater amounts than me, and she always gave me a fair price. I found her a little hard to get to know, but she kept her cards pressed close to her chest which meant it wasn't all my fault. I approached her costume jewellery display cabinet and leaned in to examine the treasure within. Several gorgeous Miriam Haskell pieces were draped over the velvet cushions. One consisted of a chain of glass, baroque, pink, pearl cabochon stones in different sizes separated by golden beads. A stunning choker and earring set of faux bridal jewellery made of blue crystals, enamel and faux pearls lay beside it. I noticed a fine collection of gilt brooches in the shape of animals. I felt a gentle pat on my shoulder and turned to find her smiling at me.

'This is an honour,' she said. 'You don't step into my lair often.'

'I brought cake,' I said. 'I thought we could have a cup of Earl Grey as it's an orange drizzle.'

'I love Ghita's cakes. They're divine. She ought to write a recipe book.'

'She's far too busy keeping Rohan and Kieron apart at the moment. I can't understand what the problem is.'

'It's probably just the stress of opening a new restaurant. January isn't exactly peak tourist season. Why don't they open it in December? They could catch the Christmas rush and try out their prices on receptive diners.'

'That's true. I haven't spoken to them since the wedding. We're all traumatised by Sharon's death. By the way, thanks for holding the fort for me. I really appreciate it.'

'I'm only sorry it ended so terribly. George must be in a terrible state. I never met Sharon, you know, and now I won't.'

''She looked just like me. We're not even sure the killer intended to murder her. D.I. Antrim still thinks I might have been the target, as unlikely as it sounds.'

'You? Why on earth would someone try and kill you?'

'Precisely. But it's a complex case. I've been investigating the set up at the hotel and every time I talk to someone, I discover more motives and more suspects.'

Grace boiled a kettle and she frowned and muttered to herself as she made the tea. I wondered if I had interrupted her at a bad time. When the tea had brewed, we sat at a table at the back of the shop sipping scalding cups of Earl Grey. Grace put down her cup and coughed.

'I'm not sure this is relevant to your investigations, but I think I met Sharon,' she said. 'Last week.'

I put down my cup and stared at her.

'Last week? Where did you meet her?'

'Here, in the shop. I thought it was you at first, from the back, but when she turned around, I realised she was, um, younger.'

I sighed.

'That sounds like her. Why did she come in?'

'She wanted to buy something for the woman who organised her wedding. She told me the woman loved old jewellery and furniture.'

'Me?'

'I guess so. I didn't put two and two together at the time, as I had several customers all wanting attention.'

'Did she buy anything?'

'A brooch. One from the collection you were admiring earlier. I'm guessing she didn't have time to give it to you.'

My head swam with possibilities.

'No, but I'm pretty sure she intended to. She told me she had a surprise for me just before she died. When I went to meet her, she had fallen to the ground after being hit on the head. She wore the same trouser suit I had on, so I assumed she wanted to show me that.'

'You didn't find any brooch at the scene?'

'I didn't look. D.I. Antrim would have had a fit if I'd touched anything. I'm a suspect, not a detective.'

'Well, you've got one more clue than they have right now. Maybe Flo can help?'

'I'll find out. Thanks.'

'My pleasure. It's a lovely brooch. I think you'd have liked it.'

I nodded and sipped my tea. Had someone taken it from the scene? I needed time to think.

Chapter 18

Sharon's funeral took place on Saturday, a week after her death. The autopsy had revealed a fractured skull and acute subdural haematoma caused by blunt force. The cause of death being so obvious, the police had released Sharon's body to her family, who had organised a service at the local crematorium. Theresa had chosen the order of service without consulting George. The Walshes treated him like a pariah. He had not been consulted on their choice of burial, nor on the inscription on her gravestone. This omission did not seem to irk him. He accepted their decisions as if they were choosing on which channel to watch the news.

'It's as if we were never together,' George told Helen. 'She's disappeared into the ether, and left me lost and confused.

Mouse had been subdued since the wedding. I suspected he was suffering from shock, but he would not discuss the event, or Sharon's death. I found a plastic bag stuffed into the dustbins outside the back door which I opened on a whim. It contained a seagull and fishing boat cot mobile from the local craft shop. I had admired one in the window walking by and even gone in to enquire about the price. I couldn't believe Mouse had bought it for Sharon's baby despite his jealousy and fear of being replaced. My heart broke for him. How must he be feeling to throw it out? I needed to talk to him after the funeral. I discreetly rescued it and hid it in the loft upstairs.

No one had thought to invite George or his relatives to the funeral, but that did not stop us all from turning up. Even Harry insisted on coming with us, as support for George. We wore black, having been sent a text by Roz who found out the dress code from her network. We travelled in two cars, mine and George's, and made the short drive to the site in weak sunshine. The red-roofed crematorium sat on the far side of the main road to Shoreham, on the crest of a small hill. Its round dome had led to it being known as the nipple, but despite the hill's genuine resemblance to a pert breast, nobody felt like repeating the joke as we approached. I had not been to a crematorium before, and I felt nervous with anticipation of the denouement of the service.

We sat in the back rows of the interior chapel, taking up two benches. A Red Sea of empty pews separated us from the Walsh and Hurley families and Sharon's few friends. Heads turned towards us and then away without a greeting. I felt like the wallflower at the school dance stranded on a bench in the gym. Then the minister arrived, dressed in a neutral grey suit. She peered at the gap between the rival factions and rolled her eyes.

'It would be nice,' she said. 'If everyone could sit closer to me, then I wouldn't have to shout.'

We all looked at each other, but nobody moved. She came down the aisle and put her hands on her hips.

'She won't take no for an answer,' hissed Helen.

We shuffled out of our pew and took the one behind the Hurleys with some reluctance. Cheaply printed orders of service had been left on the front benches. I opened mine to read the contents and couldn't help smiling. Sharon's favourite song had been 'I will survive' and nobody had thought it odd to include it in the service. Before long, the minister, who had obviously never met Sharon, began to extoll her many virtues. George snorted, making Fintan Hurley turn around and glare at him. He whispered in my ear.

'Sharon would laugh her head off if she heard this,' said George. 'She had many faults, but she knew it. At least she had the grace to be honest about it.'

'You saw a side of her we never did,' I said. 'You should treasure the good memories and forget the last revelations. I'm quite sure she loved you.'

'Probably. She just wasn't very good at it.'

I put an arm around his shoulders and felt them heave. His vulnerable inner core had been breached in the last few days and he struggled to hold it together. Helen took one of his hands and stroked it with her thumb. She gave him a shy smile. I wondered if he had the slightest inkling of her school girl crush. I found it adorable, but it seemed out of place at Sharon's funeral. I drew my eyebrows together and frowned at her. She bit her lip, but she did not relinquish George's hand.

We stood to sing 'I will survive' and it didn't seem at all funny, only bizarre. Nobody could do it justice and I felt relieved when the music ended after only two choruses. The minister bade us all to stand and then she pressed a button under the pulpit. The coffin, which had been on a set of rails at the front of the pews, trundled towards the oven. A twinge of panic rang through me. What if she were still alive? Could she escape in time? Harry held my hand tighter as he picked up my agitation. The coffin disappeared into the oven and the doors slid shut. A loud whoomph noise made everybody jump as the burners switched on.

I could not take any more and pulled myself free of Harry. I rushed outside and took a cigarette out of the packet I had bought for the wedding. I lit it and took a long drag. My heart thundered in my chest. I felt like a hypocrite. I had not even liked Sharon, and had come close to hating her, but nobody deserved to be snuffed out in the prime of life. Somebody had killed her, and I would not give up until I found them. I stamped on the cigarette, annoyed I had smoked so soon after the last one. A metal bin stood on the side of the path and I threw the cigarettes into it. Then I took out a packet of Polo mints and chewed two in quick succession. Who would I fool with that old chestnut? I knew I would stink anyway.

Theresa burst out of the door. Tears streamed down her face, cutting canyons through her perfect white makeup. She looked startled to find me outside the church.

'You gave me a fright,' she said. 'Do you make a habit of hanging around church doors? I saw you hiding, you know. At the wedding. I know you heard us.'

'So what if I did? It doesn't make any difference now, does it?'

'What do you mean?'

'George will keep his property. Sharon didn't win in the end.'

Theresa's face turned purple with rage.

'She's dead, you old cow. My sister's dead, and you're talking about winning.'

She had every right to get hysterical, but I couldn't help myself.

'Sharon never loved George,' I said. 'She pretended to be pregnant to steal his money. What do you expect me to feel?'

'Sympathy, perhaps. I lost my sister, and my husband has hit the bottle. The business is collapsing.'

Her ravaged face showed through the mask of makeup. Guilt invaded every pore of my being. How would I feel if Helen died like that? I took her arm and turned to face her.

'I apologise for being obnoxious. I'm terribly sorry for your loss. And George's. I'm finding this incredibly difficult, so I can't imagine how it is for you. Please excuse my callousness. It's quite unforgiveable.'

She looked into my eyes, trying to read them for deception or exaggeration but found none. Her expression softened.

'It must be so weird for you. You were good to organise the wedding and help Sharon out. She felt bewildered by your kindness after all the pain she caused you. I feel like you might have become friends without all of this.'

She gestured at the crematorium.

'I had that feeling too,' I said. 'I'm investigating her death, you know. The local police force is at sixes and sevens with it, but I have different leads to them. Would you consent to talking about your business and so on? It might help me find out who did this. It may even have been an accident.'

'I heard about you, and your sleuthing activities. Fintan says you're nothing but an interfering busybody who thinks being married to a policeman gave you magic powers.'

She smirked and I wanted to retort, but she held up her hand.

'I'm not sure it's possible to change his mind, but I can try,' she said. 'I'll speak to you next week sometime. Have you got my mobile number?'

I shook my head. She tapped it out on my phone for me and then took me by the arm.

'We're going to the pub for a wake. Will you have a drink with us?'

Before I could answer, Harry and George came out of the crematorium, followed by Mouse and Helen and the other mourners. George stared at the two of us, still arm in arm, for a few seconds, before striding off after the rest.

'Women,' he muttered.

Chapter 19

We did not stay for long at the wake. Despite our good intentions, the atmosphere quickly became toxic as Fintan began to sound off about the police force and their inability to catch the killer of his sister-in-law. He pretended to be making a general point, but I could see his comments were cutting George to the quick. Harry puffed up his chest in protest at the implied criticism of his friend, and I sensed everything might go rapidly downhill if we didn't leave. I poked Helen in the ribs and indicated the door with a flick of my head. She had been struggling with excruciating social panic and her shoulders sagged with relief when she acknowledged my signal. I looked around for Mouse and found him standing out in the passageway near the toilets. He had tears in his eyes.

'Can we go home now please?' he said. 'I don't think I can bear another minute of this.'

I didn't need any further incentive. I told him to leave the pub and wait in the car while I rounded up the others. Helen pulled George away from Fintan as they had started to size each other up. I noticed Harry covered their exit, which made me smile. He could not shed his army habit of always looking after his 'men'. I shrugged and waved at Theresa, and made a telephone sign at her, mouthing 'call me' without any hope she would actually do so. We hadn't managed to speak in the pub, due to the two factions separating to different sides of the room and glaring at each other. It felt like a scene from West Side Story.

Nobody spoke on the way home. Harry patted my leg and twisted in his seat to speak to Mouse, but Mouse stared out of the window pretending not to see him. We got home in one piece. I looked around for George's car, but it hadn't arrived. I texted Helen to ask if they were alright, and she answered to tell me that she and George drove straight to home, despite saying they would come to the Grotty Hovel first. I didn't ask why.

Harry went upstairs to have a bath and I sat on the sofa with Mouse. Hades went straight to Mouse and purred into his ear. I swear he understands Mouse as well as any human. Tears fell on his fur as Mouse struggled to control his feelings.

'I didn't even like her,' he said. 'Why am I so sad?'

'We're all sad, sweetheart. George has infected us with his grief because we love him. We're all feeling guilty because we didn't like her much. It's hard to believe she lied about the baby. You and I were looking forward to it. We're in mourning for the lost opportunities.'

'Are we going to find the murderer?'

'I don't know if there is one yet. This may be a terrible accident. We need to keep open minds.'

'Will I feel better if it was an accident?'

'You might.'

He brightened at the thought, sitting up and making Hades jump off him in faux panic.

'Can I help? Please give me something to do. I feel so useless, and Dad is so destroyed.'

Mouse hardly ever referred to George as Dad. He mostly called him George or my father. The depth of feeling he had experienced for George had shocked him, but in a small way, he also seemed relieved to realise they still loved each other.

'I'm going to meet Theresa to talk about Sharon. Would you like to do some background research on their business? I never understood what they did. Perhaps there is a disgruntled supplier or client we don't know about. They could have killed Sharon and left through the doors to the main building without anyone seeing them. That reminds me, can you find out if the hotel has CCTV feed we can examine? Tim Boulting is not keen on any investigation, but maybe Dermot can help us get access to recordings of the wedding.'

'Okay. I can do that.'

'Why don't you go upstairs and have a nap? A bit of quiet time might be good for you before supper. You can take Hades up with you if you want, but leave the door open in case he wants to go out later.'

I went into the kitchen and opened the fridge. Then I closed it again. I had bought a chicken for supper, but the idea of cooking anything in the oven made me feel sick. My cell phone started to vibrate on the kitchen table. I picked it up and saw George's number.

'Are you okay?' I said. 'We're worried about you.'

'Can I talk to you?' he said. 'I need to clear the air.'

'Okay. Do you want to come over here?'

'No. Helen says you like to sit in the wind shelter.'

'I do, usually, but it's dark outside and freezing cold.'

'Please, Tan.'

I sighed.

'All right. I'll be there in five minutes. Do you want me to bring a flask of tea?'

'Can you put a tot of whisky in it?'

'I can.'

I put on the kettle and took down the pot. I made the tea strong, like George liked it and added milk and a tot to the flask. Then I put on my heavy winter coat, my cashmere beanie and scarf, my heavy-duty gloves and grabbed my keys. As I opened the front door Harry appeared, towelling his hair dry.

'Where on earth are you going?' he said.

'George,' I said. 'He wants to talk. Will you peel the spuds for me, please. I'll be back soon.'

He shrugged.

'Okay. Don't freeze to death out there. Herbert and his friends will eat you.'

I gave him a tiny smile and let myself out. The northeast wind almost froze my eyeballs in their sockets. I pulled the hood of the coat over the beanie and half of my face with the result that I couldn't see where I was going. I walked straight into a wheelie bin and almost fell flat on my face. Luckily, I didn't drop the flask. Gathering what was left of my dignity, I headed for the shelter. I could see George's solid frame through the glass partition. He had the typical male habit of underestimating the cold and I realised I might have to part with some of my central heating to stop him going into a coma.

'Hi, Tan,' he said. 'Thanks for coming. Is that the tea?'

I poured him a cup before sitting down and passed him my beloved purple beanie and scarf. He looked rather ludicrous in them, but at least the colour had returned to his face.

'Ah, nectar,' he said, slurping his tea.

'What do you want? I'm supposed to be making supper.'

He handed me the cup.

'Have some tea,' he said. 'This is important, or I wouldn't have called you out on a night like this. It's about Tarton Manor House.'

I sipped the tea and waited.

'You know you asked me about why I went there before the wedding?'

'I remember.'

'Look, I'm sorry I blew you off. You caught me off guard. I didn't know anyone had seen me.'

'So why did you go there?'

'It's embarrassing.'

'More embarrassing than being arrested for murder?'

He rolled his eyes.

'Almost. I had doubts about the wedding. I wanted to call it off, but I went there to think. And then it reminded me…'

He tailed off and waved his hands in the air.

'Reminded you of what?' I said.

'You, of course. I had such a clear vision of our wedding. Our parents. Our friends. The happiness. It seemed like such a contrast with what would come with Sharon and her dreadful relatives. I felt trapped, but whether by the past or the future, I couldn't tell you. I had to sit down for a while and recover my bearings. I could hear the music and hear the laughter, your laughter, Tan.'

His confession hit me hard. I had also experienced those memories on my visit. I never expected him to recall stuff like that.

'Did you see anyone you recognised at the hotel?'

'That day? No, I don't think so. Obviously, someone saw me, but I didn't see them, or if I did, I didn't know them.'

'We're working on a theory that Sharon's death may have been accidental,' I said. 'Or at least unexpected.'

'What can you tell me about it?'

'It may be something to do with an insurance scam, but we're not sure yet. We haven't counted Fintan out yet.'

George folded his lips inwards, a sure sign he had something he wanted to say. I waited as the cold crept into my toes and up my boots.

'When Sharon told me about losing the baby, I felt cheated and furious. I didn't want to listen to her anymore. But she had also kept something back which she promised to tell me after the wedding. At the time, I dismissed it as more lies, but her tone should have alerted me.'

'What do you mean?'

'I'm not sure. She seemed worried, but maybe she just wanted to distract me. I don't know.'

'Neither do I.'

I sighed and he patted my leg.

'By the way, Flo called me. The house is clear. I can move back in tomorrow. Will you come with me? I'm not sure I can go in alone.'

'What did Helen say?'

'About me leaving? She's gone upstairs to her room.'

'She'll miss you. She enjoyed fussing over you.'

'She's an angel, but I've got to go home and sort out my head. Will you come?'

'Of course.'

'Who knows what we'll find there? I'll pick you up in the morning.'

Chapter 20

The next morning, I got up early to be ready for George. In his book, nine o'clock counted as mid-morning, so I wanted to prevent him having to wait for me and getting impatient. Harry went downstairs to make me breakfast while I had a shower. He cooked us scrambled eggs with a knob of butter and a pinch of salt and pepper. As I came down the stairs, he loaded up some freshly buttered toast with the eggs and put them on the table.

'Eat up. You don't want to be late,' he said.

I gave him a big sloppy kiss and sat down to eat. The eggs were so delicious, I couldn't help making appreciative noises. Harry laughed.

'Were you hungry?' he said.

'I'm always hungry. Don't laugh at me.'

'I'm so thrilled you love your food. I've broken up with people for pushing a lettuce leaf around a plate before.'

I grinned.

'Thank you for breakfast. I'm not sure what we'll find in George's house. He needs me.'

'I know. My ego is not so fragile that I'm worried about you helping him. I've got to do my final penance with Grace today, but I'll be back this evening to my family, you and Mouse and Hades.'

'Don't get all sentimental on me. I'm not jealous of Grace either.'

'You are a little.'

I laughed.

'Not even a teeny-weeny bit.'

Then I remembered my conversation with Grace about the brooch Sharon had bought, presumably for me. The strong emotions surrounding the funeral had pushed it to the back of my mind. I made a mental note to ask Flo about it. The doorbell rang and I grabbed my shoulder bag.

'Have a great day. And feed the cat and the Mouse if you've got time.'

'Will do.'

George helped me on with my coat and we left the Grotty Hovel to jump into his car, which he had left with the engine running. My street did not qualify as a hub of crime, but I found it odd a policeman would leave his keys in the ignition.

'Are you okay?' I said, as I put on my seatbelt.

'I don't know if I'll ever be okay again,' said George.

We drove to the house where we used to live together. I hadn't been back since George and I had divorced, and he had bought the Grotty Hovel for me to live in. His mother dying had been a Godsend for me in terms of what we could afford after the breakup. We both found it easier to be civil when we could move into a house each. George kept the villa, which was his pride and joy. He loved the plain, neutral decoration of the rooms. He never let me have any 'bits of junk' on the shelves. Everything had to be brand new. He even bought some revolting modern figurines to encourage me. I broke one on purpose in a fit of pique while dusting the shelves. I had grown to loath the beige villa almost as much as I now loved the Grotty Hovel, with its lovely eclectic assortment of vintage finds and its grumpy cat. Even George seemed to like visiting us more than he admitted.

The beige villa sat in a modern housing estate in the suburbs of Seacastle, not that the town really merited them. Most people bought a villa to avoid paying top dollar in Brighton and commuted there instead. The tyres popped and crunched on the gravel in the short driveway, a sound which brought back memories of miserable homecomings, after I'd disappointed George in some way. I later realised I couldn't do anything right because my name wasn't Sharon, but at the time, I felt useless and extra. I got out of the car and waited for him to open the front door. Lengths of police tape had been crumpled up into a ball and dumped in the porch. The yellow mass seemed to irritate George, who picked it up, muttering.

I followed him into the house which did not look materially different to when I had left it. Some bland rugs and sand-coloured cushions had invaded the lounge, but Sharon had obviously had the same taste as George, or she didn't care enough to put her mark on the place. I felt a twinge of regret for her passing. Whatever she had done, it didn't deserve this. Someone had rubbed her off the face off the planet for no good reason. George stopped in the middle of the room, his face pale.

'I can still smell her,' he said. 'I don't think I can go into our bedroom. If I stay downstairs and revise papers here, can you have a look upstairs? Just in case, the SOCO missed something.'

I nodded and set off up the stairs. A strong sense of déjà vu hit me as I entered our former bedroom. It smelled different now, but it still made the hairs on my arms stand erect as I scanned the familiar wardrobe and chest of drawers. SOCO had emptied all the drawers onto the bed. I suspected their respect for George had made them leave the room tidier than usual. His shirts and suits had all been piled up on the arm chair. I decided not to waste my time looking through the clothes. I opened the wardrobe and looked in. Nothing remained inside. Then I looked in the bottom drawer which was also empty. I had purposely left the side tables until last, but they had also been stripped of their contents. I noticed a pile of assorted items on the floor. Pill bottles, bookmarks, charger cords, scrunchies and polo mints, the debris of a life cut short. Then I spotted a receipt. It had been neatly folded and used as a bookmark in a women's fiction book. It was made out for an Art Deco brooch from Grace and Max Wong's antique shop.

I put it in my wallet, intending to take it to Flo. The brooch might well turn out to be important in the case. I couldn't believe SOCO hadn't removed it. Maybe they had thought it unimportant.

'How's it going up there?' said George, from the bottom of the stairs.

'What would you like me to do with Sharon's clothes? Shall I put them back into the cupboards?'

'I don't know. Do you want them?'

'No, but Theresa might. I can ask her to come and collect them if you want to bag them up.'

'That's a good idea. Sharon really didn't have much stuff. I always wondered why she had so little.'

'Can you bring up Sharon's suitcases from the garage? We can put the stuff in them.'

'I don't think I can face it yet. Can you move my clothes into the spare room and then shut the main bedroom. I'll deal with it when I'm able.'

It wasn't only Sharon who had a limited number of personal items. It only took me four trips to transfer George's suits and shirts to the spare room's wardrobe, and his underwear and tee shirts to the drawers. It felt so personal to be touching his belongings again. Out of habit I brought his suits up to my nose and sniffed them. They had that coffee stained, musty odour from long hours at the office. I used to have them dry cleaned regularly, but they had food stains and sticky patches on them. The neglect made me nostalgic for our former life when I sent him out clean and fed to work no matter how bad the depression hit that day. In a way it had kept me going when I no longer cared about anything, not even my own job. I sighed. What would he do now? I looked around for any more of his gear. His sports gear had been stuffed into a holdall. It wasn't like he used it much, but I transferred it too.

When I had finished, I shut the door of the master bedroom and turned the key. I left it on the side table of the spare bed and went back downstairs. George sat on the couch surrounded by paperwork. A child's painting had been propped up against one of the sand-coloured cushions. It showed a man and a boy playing with a kite. George had never played with Mouse if he could avoid it. I wondered where Mouse had got the idea to paint such a scene. George saw me glance at the painting.

'I was a terrible husband, and not much of a father either,' he said. 'I don't know why I thought it would be different with Sharon.'

'You still have time to be a great father. Mouse loves you.'

He sighed and gesticulated at the papers.

'None of this belonged to Sharon,' he said. 'This is all mine. I guess they took photographs of the letters that interested them. They already have our laptops.'

'What about Sharon's accounts?' I said. 'Where did she keep them?'

'Probably on the laptop. You'll have to ask Theresa. Sharon wouldn't tell me much about their business.'

'It sounds like we should talk to her together.'

'If you like, although I'm not sure she'd tell me anything. Her husband isn't keen on the police.'

'So I heard. Look, if it's okay with you, I'll meet her without you then. I promise to tell you anything important I find out.'

George waved his hands in the air.

'If anyone can find out what happened, it's you. I don't trust Antrim as far as I can throw him. He's made it pretty clear I'm still a suspect.'

'Can you drop me off at the shop? I really need to get some Christmas decorating done.'

Chapter 21

The Second Home welcomed me into its chilly interior as I fought to shut the door against a stiff breeze coming off the sea. It filled the shop with the smell of seaweed and fresh mornings. Roz stood behind the counter in a leather jacket and fingerless gloves looking like an extra from a Madonna movie. She had dyed her hair green. I couldn't keep track of the changes. If I had made a hair diary, I might have been able to predict her moods better, but it seemed unlikely.

'What time do you call this?' she said.

I shrugged.

'The dog ate my homework.'

'A likely story.'

She came around the counter and gave me a hug, examining my face and the dark bags under my eyes.

'Are you okay? Ghita told me you went to your old house with George. That must have been weird.'

'You have no idea how strange the last few days have been. The funeral spooked me out. And Sharon's family are so aggressive. Poor Mouse is completely traumatised. The visit to George's house was the icing on the cake.'

'Would you like a latte?'

'You can't imagine how much.'

'I'll nip down the street and get some milk. Ghita wanted to see you too. I'll bring her back with me.'

I did not feel in the mood for a get together, but Roz and Ghita were my favourite sounding boards. I needed to think aloud to plan my next move. I climbed the stairs and sat in the window seat overlooking the high street. A lone sea gull whirled above the shop emitting screeching cries and scouring the landscape for an easy meal. I thought about George sitting alone amid the ruins of his life in the beige villa. He needed his life back. I texted Helen and asked her to take him some essentials for his fridge. Knowing him, it contained a red pepper and half a pint of sour milk.

Downstairs the doorbell clanged and my friends came in, chatting and giggling. It lifted my spirits to hear them despite my reluctance. I moved to the banquette beside the Gaggia. Ghita came over and hugged me. She smelled of patchouli and spices and sesame oil. She stroked my hair.

'I know seeing George get married must have been tough, but you didn't need to murder the bride.'

A smile played on her face and I couldn't help laughing.

'Ghita Chowdhury! Have you been practicing your black humour?' said Roz.

'Try working with Rohan and Kieron. I had to learn to defend myself.'

'Honestly, this whole week has been a nightmare. If it hadn't been for Helen taking George in, I don't know how we'd have coped,' I said.

Roz's eyes lit up. I could see her gossip antennae flickering.

'George stayed with Helen? It's bad enough you organising his wedding, without your sister replacing his wife.'

'It's not like that at all, Roz. We had to throw all hands to the pump.'

Roz looked at Ghita and they both burst out laughing. I realised what I'd said and joined in. The cares of the past week lifted a little.

'Can you please stop making dirty jokes and listen? I've discovered an insurance fraud at the hotel which may be related to the accident.'

'Accident? I thought it was murder?' said Ghita.

'Well, it's complicated. It could have been murder. Or an accident. Or someone murdered the wrong person by accident...'

'Blimey,' said Roz. 'It hasn't got any simpler then?'

'Not really. And to top it off, Grace sold Sharon a brooch intended for me, and I think someone stole it at the wedding.'

'From you?' said Ghita.

'No. From Sharon. Possibly as she lay dying,' I said. 'I told you it was complicated.'

'I'll make you a latte,' said Roz.

'Is it too early for cake?' said Ghita. 'I made a Granny Chowdhury fruit cake.'

'It's never too early for cake. I'll call it lunch though.'

We all settled down with our coffees and munched our way through a fat slice of slightly spiced fruit cake.

'This is heavenly,' I said. 'You definitely need to make a recipe book. Mouse could help you with the formatting.'

'I'd love to, but wouldn't it be ridiculously expensive?'

'Mouse knows places which print on demand. He can find out.'

'Did Mouse discover the insurance scam on the net?' said Roz.

'Actually, your cousin Dermot told him about it. We suspect the former owner, Lydia Sheldon may have been tempted to precipitate an accident, in order for the Tippings to lose their insurance. It's a long story.'

'But if no one can insure the hotel afterwards, how does that help?'

'Ah, Lydia Sheldon may have uncovered proof that the subsidence was invented to get permission to knock down an oak tree on the grounds. So, if the hotel first loses its insurance, she can pick it up for a song and then reinsure it without subsidence.'

'How is Sharon's death related to the scheme?'

'Someone had levered the flower pot off its new cement on the balcony.'

'On purpose?'

'We don't know. They may have only intended to injure someone to give the insurance company a reason to cancel their policy.'

'How will you find out?'

'I'm not sure yet. We need to establish who loosened the pot. They may not be the same person who pushed it off the balcony.'

'And what if the person who did that thought it was you walking underneath it, and not Sharon?'

'I've considered that. The only person I know who wanted to cancel me out, or scare me off, was Fintan, Sharon's brother-in-law.'

'Fintan? But why would he want to do that?'

'I heard him talking to Theresa about Sharon stringing George along. Fintan spotted me listening, so he may have been trying to silence me to stop me telling George the truth about his wife.'

'And you were wearing the same clothes, so he could have mistaken Sharon for you,' said Roz.

'The same clothes?' said Ghita.

'Sharon changed into a going away trouser suit. The make and colour were the same as the one I wore to the wedding. And we do look similar,' I said.

'That's an awful lot of loose ends,' said Ghita.

'Can we do anything to help?' said Roz.

'I don't think so, but listening helps.'

'You haven't told us why the brooch is relevant,' said Ghita.

'I don't know that it is yet. Whoever took it may have had nothing to do with the murder.'

'And how do you know they took it? Maybe it's still in one of the changing rooms,' said Roz. 'Why don't we go and check? We can have a search for the chisel while we are there. Maybe the person who used it was forced to hide it nearby.'

'What about the shop?' I said.

Roz looked around with her hand faux-shielding her eyes.

'We don't seem to have any customers right now.'

'I can keep shop for an hour or two, if you promise to tell me all about it,' said Ghita. 'The boys are going to Brighton to talk to an investor about a bridging loan.'

'I hope they're going to open before they run out of money,' said Roz. 'They are the kings of delay.'

'That's what happens when a procrastinator meets a perfectionist,' said Ghita. 'I stay well out of it. As long as they can pay me, I'm quite happy.'

'About that,' I said.

'Don't worry, sweetheart, this is on me,' said Ghita.

I beamed at her.

'If you get bored, I left more decorations for the shop in a box near the kitchenette.'

'How exciting. I love decorating for Christmas.'

'Let me check my phone in case Ed needs anything before we set out,' said Roz, scrolling.

Her eyes lit up.

'You'll never guess what. Dermot sent me a text asking us to come up to Tarton. He's found something we might be interested in.'

'What are we waiting for?'

Chapter 22

I drove Roz to Tarton Manor House between hedges decked in hoar frost. The fields behind them retained their plough furrows which stood rigid in the freezing air. A fox slunk along beside the hedge, hardly bothering to hide when we passed her. She looked thin and dirty. I crossed my fingers she would find a plump hibernating vole in her hunt. As we drove up the drive to the hotel, it became obvious that an incident of some sort had occurred. An ambulance stood outside the main door and I spotted D.I. Antrim's car lurking near the bushes. Two paramedics carried a stretcher toward the open back doors of the ambulance.

I considered turning around and driving off, but D.I. Antrim had chosen the same moment to emerge from the hotel for a smoke. When he spotted my car, he rolled his eyes and pointed out a parking space with a stiff finger. I got the hint.

'Awkward,' said Roz.

'Typical, more like. I think he has a tracker on my car. How did he know I'd be coming.'

'I expect he's asking himself the same question about you,' said Roz.

I sighed. We approached him with trepidation, but he forced out a grim smile.

'Ms Bowe. And Ms Murray, isn't it? I don't suppose you've come for afternoon tea?'

'If you're inviting, I'm game,' said Roz.

'I presume you're following a lead,' said Antrim. 'I'll stand you a cup of tea if you want to talk about what just happened here. I feel an exchange of information could be timely.'

'Throw in a biscuit and it's a deal,' I said.

He sighed.

'Come on then.'

I glanced into the ambulance and saw the soles of two muddy wellingtons.

'Who's on the stretcher?'

'The gardener, Dermot something. A person or persons unknown knocked him out.'

Roz gasped and held her head in her hands.

'He's my cousin. We were coming to see him. Is he going to be okay?'

'I don't know. He took quite a blow to the head. Will you go with him in the ambulance?'

'Of course. I'm sorry, Tan. It's an emergency.'

I gave her a kiss and she went over to the paramedics who let her ride in the back with Dermot as they drove off. Shaken by events, I hardly noticed D.I. Antrim leading me through the lobby of the hotel and into the tea rooms. I sat catatonic while he ordered tea and biscuits and waited for me to come down to earth.

'Ms Bowe?' he said. 'Can you tell me what Dermot wanted?'

'He texted Roz a little earlier and told her he had found something important for the investigation. We were coming anyway, but—'

'Why were you coming?'

'We intended to search the changing rooms for a brooch, and maybe a chisel.'

He raised an eyebrow. The waiter approached with a tray carrying a large pot of tea and some boring-looking biscuits. Honestly, at their prices I had expected chocolate ones, not plain. I let Antrim pour as I couldn't guarantee to avoid sloshing tea everywhere. My nerves were shot by the downing of poor Dermot.

'You're going to have to explain the brooch,' he said.

'As far as I can make out, Sharon bought a brooch from Grace Wong's shop to give to me for organising the wedding. I have the receipt right here. I meant to bring it over to the station today.'

I fished in my handbag for my wallet and removed the receipt which I handed to him.

'We didn't find any brooch at the crime scene,' he said.

'SOCO didn't know they should look for it. Roz and I thought we might find it hidden in one of the changing rooms or the toilet. Whoever stole it may not have had the time or courage to smuggle it out yet.'

'And the chisel?'

'The hotel manager told us he had recently paid for the gargoyle flower pots to be recemented in place. Somebody must have used a chisel to prise one of them off again. We're working on the theory that the pot had been prepared for easy pushing before the wedding.'

'And why is that?'

'Because the toilets and changing rooms are always busy at a wedding. There's no way someone could chisel the flower pot loose during dinner without someone seeing them.'

D.I. Antrim dunked a biscuit in his tea holding it there while he considered this. He waited too long and half of it fell into his cup with a splash. I hid a smirk.

'That makes sense. Maybe Dermot came across a chisel in the garden?'

'It's possible. Where did they find him?'

'Flat on his back in the flower bed. We can go and check shortly. Drink your tea first.'

The tea turned out to be hot enough to strip paint. I blew on the surface, making ripples across the cup while I let my mind wander. Tim Boulting, the hotel manager came over to our table, all shiny and obsequious.

'I hope the tea is to your satisfaction, Inspector. It's a special blend that we have sent direct from Twinings. We sell it in the foyer, if you're interested.'

A look of annoyance ghosted across D.I. Antrim's face.

'It's too hot to drink so far,' he said, lips pursed. 'You should take out insurance in case a guest scalds themselves to death.'

A lightbulb went on somewhere in the labyrinth of my brain.

'What's the name of the insurance company that covers this hotel?' I asked.

'I hardly think that's relevant,' said Boulting.

'Oh, I think it is,' said Antrim, putting down his cup and fixing Boulting with a steely glare.

Boulting blanched and a bead of sweat trickled down his temple. He took out a revolting handkerchief and mopped it up. He licked his lips.

'Safe Haven,' he said. 'We've been with them for years.'

'Have you now?' said Antrim. 'Won't they cancel the insurance after the incident last week?'

'Not if it's a deliberate act. We're relying on you to find the culprit.'

'I'd better get on with it then.'

Boulting made a faintly ridiculous half bow and backed away from the table. As I watched him slide out of the room, the name of the insurance company rang bells in my brain. Then I had it. Lydia Sheldon. I couldn't believe it. I took my notebook out of my handbag and flipped back through the pages until I found the reference. The same company who insured her husband before he died of a heart attack. When I looked up, Terry Antrim was watching me with amusement playing in his eyes. It was not the first time I had been struck by the animal magnetism that prowled behind them. I felt like a small rodent being played by a cat.

'We'd better get looking then,' I said, trying to drink my tea.

The scalding liquid raised a blister in my mouth but I couldn't drink it fast enough with his gaze burning a hole in my confidence.

'Are you going to tell me why you looked in your notebook like a female Poirot when Boulting mentioned the insurance company?'

I sighed.

'Sure.'

I filled him in on the whole Lydia Sheldon angle. He listened with rapt attention, making notes in his Rite-in-Rain notebook with a propelling pencil. As I told him, I realised something I had not considered.

'She called Sharon's death an unfortunate accident. But most people were, and are, under the impression that someone murdered Sharon on purpose. Why did Lydia assume it had been an accident? She said something about Karma too,' I said.

'A dangerous woman with a massive axe to grind. Could she be responsible for the accident?'

'She didn't come to the wedding. But she could have sent someone or known one of the attendees.'

'Sharon's relatives are a rough bunch, and some of them have criminal records,' said Antrim.

'I know, but who would kill someone from their family on their wedding day?'

'The insurance company may be the key to all this. From what you say, the Tippings swindled Lydia out of her home, and then pretended the oak tree had caused subsidence in order to remove it. I can't see how they did it without the cooperation of someone in the company.'

'But they shot themselves in the foot because the insurance company can use the slightest excuse to stop insuring the hotel,' I said, my excitement rising.

Antrim drummed his fingers on the table.

'I smell blackmail,' he said. 'Tim Boulting seems to me like a man under pressure. I'll call him in for questioning. Meanwhile, can you get that son of yours to have a discreet look for connections between the Tippings and Safe Haven? I don't want to alert them by using official channels.'

'Of course. Mouse will be ecstatic. He's desperate to help his father.'

'Leave the tea. It's revolting anyway. Let's go and search the hotel.'

Chapter 23

Antrim led the way to the flowerbed where Dermot had been found. He had been spreading mulch on the rose beds along the short block joining the conservatory to the main building. The fresh wood chips stopped abruptly about half way along and a spade had been dropped, scattering some of them randomly on the surface. Dermot's footprints stood out in the wet soil. I wondered if he had revived yet. Roz had turned as white as snow with fright when she realised he had been attacked. I sent her a quick text asking her how they were both doing. I also rang Ghita and told her to close the shop so she could give her Fat Fighters' class. I did not elaborate on why, but I gathered she had already spoken to Roz as she did not question my decision.

'I'm guessing whoever knocked him out also removed whatever he had found,' I said, after we had poked around the rose bed for a few minutes. 'Roz will text us if he says anything.'

'Are those the male changing room's windows?' said Antrim. 'We should go up and look around.'

I followed him to the front door where Boulting blocked our entrance.

'I'm sorry,' he said. 'But I can't have you traipsing all that mud through the lobby. Can you put on some hotel slippers? I'll get the porter to clean your shoes for you.'

Antrim rolled his eyes, but he took off his shoes and handed them to the porter. I did the same. I noticed Antrim's big toe poking through his sock and felt sorry for him. Did he not have a Mrs Antrim to do that for him, if he couldn't do it himself? He shoved his feet into the slippers which were made of a garish white waffle material. Mine were too small for me, but I didn't complain. I looked around the lobby and took in the Christmas decorations I hadn't noticed before, in my fright at the assault on Dermot. I stared up the split staircase with garlands of fake ivy and berries intertwined in the banisters, almost walking into a huge festive Christmas tree in the corner. Antrim took my shoulders and steered me towards the swinging doors to the right of the lobby which led into the extension block with the toilets and changing rooms. I avoided treading on the floor where Sharon had died by skirting around it. The stain had been removed from the parquet floor, but not my memory.

We mounted the stairs to the men's changing room. I went straight to the window when I entered, and opened the catch. As it swung open, I leaned out and looked down to the ground. I could see the newly laid wood chips in the rose bed below.

'This is it,' I said. 'Whatever Dermot found down there; somebody must have dropped it out of this window.'

'I'd place bets on them dropping a chisel. Perhaps whoever loosened the flower pot got disturbed in the act, and got rid of it to avoid questions. He or she probably intended to return and collect the chisel from the rose bed later.'

'But Dermot found it instead. Who on earth knocked him out though? How did they know what he had found. Maybe he told someone who had reasons to get rid of the evidence?' I said.

'That's a possibility. SOCO already searched this changing room. But it's worth having a look in the other one.'

We descended into the passageway. Before going down, I couldn't help noticing the space that used to contain the gargoyle flower pot. It reminded me of the gap left when a child's tooth falls out. The pot's companion sat impassive on the balcony edge, surveying us with a hideous grimace on its face. It could have told us the whole story if we'd done the Piertotum Locomotor spell from Harry Potter. Unfortunately, I'm a muggle and, although Antrim looked like he should have been put in Slytherin, he did not seem like someone who enjoyed magic. He looked at his phone.

'Ah, they didn't check it. We'll have to get suited up.'

I didn't mind taking off my shoes, but the thought of putting on a SOCO overall again brought back bad memories of the gloating female officer who supervised me the first time. However, my curiosity overcame my reluctance, so I accepted a suit and entered the women's toilet to change. The smell of lavender brought back more memories of the wedding and the conversation I overheard in the toilet between Theresa and Sharon. Had Sharon wanted to back out on their scheme to swindle George? What if Fintan had got wind of her change of mind? Antrim knocked on the door. An impatient knock. I could almost feel his irritation. I pulled the zip up on my suit and pulled the shoe covers over my slippers.

He rolled his eyes as I emerged.

'Honestly, how long does it take to change into an overall,' he said, handing me a pair of gloves.

'You sound like a jaded husband,' I said. 'I'm here now. Let's go up.'

'I'm waiting for Tim Boulting.'

My turn to roll my eyes.

'What does he have to do with anything?'

'He's got the key.'

Tim Boulting made us wait. When he eventually turned up, he handed over the key with great reluctance.

'Don't damage the fittings. It cost us a fortune to refurbish last time,' he said.

'We'll do whatever's necessary,' said Antrim, and started up the stairs.

I followed him, giving Boulting a smug smile over my shoulder. He glared at me, and stayed put. Antrim pushed the door open with his gloved hand. The room looked identical to the men's one opposite. An open cupboard with empty hangers stood against one wall and a tartan sofa on the other.

'Let's have a look for the brooch,' he said.

There weren't many places to search. The wardrobe didn't have any nooks or crannies where you could hide an object. The walls and ceiling were empty except for a picture of a Scottish castle beside a loch with highland cattle browsing nearby. Antrim removed the painting and searched behind it. I pulled the seat cushions off the sofa and stuck my gloved hand down the seams. I felt something crinkle under my fingertips.

'There's something here,' I said. 'But I can't reach it.'

'Let me try.'

He stuck his long thin fingers into the gap and pulled out a piece of white crepe paper and a red ribbon. He reinserted his gloved hand and felt around. A smile crept onto his lips as he pulled out a miniature envelope. Somebody had written Tanya on it. He opened the envelope with exaggerated care and drew out a tiny card. He handed it to me.

'Read it,' he said.

A shiver ran up my spine. I opened the card and read the careful script out loud.

'Tan. Thank you for organising our wedding. George told me Art Deco is your favourite. Sharon.'

I almost lost it. Sharon had not only bought me a gift; she had written me a lovely note. George had never shown a single inkling of knowing anything about my tastes. He never bought me presents on my birthday or for Christmas. He just gave me his credit card and told me to buy something nice for myself in a condescending way. How did he know I liked Art Deco? I bit my lip and waited for Antrim to say something.

'Was the brooch Art Deco?' he said.

'Yes, by Miriam Haskell, a well-known designer.'

'Expensive?'

'Grace only sells high end antiques.'

'Would someone have killed for it?'

I blinked.

'I don't know. I'm not sure, but I shouldn't think so. Those Art Deco pieces are made of glass, not precious stones. Grace told me the brooch had the form of a lizard. They were made for novelty value. People collect them.'

He nodded and held out his hand. He carefully inserted the card back into the envelope. Then he took out a small plastic Ziploc bag and placed it inside with the crepe paper and the ribbon.

'There are blood spots on the crepe paper. We may be able to get samples of DNA from them and maybe from the paper itself.'

Then he took photographs of the sofa and the cushions which we then replaced. I wanted to sit down, but I knew I might contaminate the evidence.

'I'd like to go now,' I said.

He looked at me with concern.

'You're as pale as a ghost. Let's go to the squad car. There's a flask of proper tea down there.'

As we passed through the front hall, the porter gave our shoes back to us, polished to a military shine.

'Wow! Thank you so much. These are amazing. Can I bring all my shoes to you for a clean?'

He beamed.

'Mr Boulting said the same thing.'

My cell phone vibrated in my pocket and I pulled it out and read the message.

'Dermot says it was a chisel. He didn't see anyone approach him. They hit him from behind.'

I passed it to Antrim to read as I hopped around trying to pull my bootees back on. He nodded and handed it back.

'We'll send someone to get a statement tomorrow. Are you ready for a cup of lukewarm, over-strong tea?'

Chapter 24

On my way home from the hotel I pondered the information we had accumulated from our visit. It seemed to make a connection to the hotel scam less certain, although it remained in the running. Who had taken the brooch? They must have picked it up off the ground where Sharon lay dying. Did they rush upstairs to avoid detection when they saw me coming? And where was Boulting at the time? If he saw them, wouldn't he have told the police? Unless he had pushed the flower pot, and the theft had been an opportunistic one perpetrated by someone else. My head whirled with possibilities.

D.I. Antrim had promised to keep me informed as much as possible, on condition I did the same. Mouse would be pleased to use his skills and be involved in the case. I like the fact Antrim had been pragmatic about our involvement. I supposed he didn't really have a choice. At least he hadn't mentioned George once in connection with the murder. This may have been because he intended to keep his cards close to his chest, but I didn't believe that.

I arrived home to find Harry and Mouse in the kitchen. They had roasted a chicken and the fabulous smell hit me as I opened the front door, making me salivate. I realised just how long it had been since I had eaten anything resembling a cooked meal. Harry rushed out to greet me.

'Are you all right, darling? Roz told me of the dramas at Tarton Manor House.'

'I can't believe someone would hurt Dermot,' said Mouse. 'Do we know if he is going to be okay?'

I reassured him and showed him Roz's message.

'Are you hungry?' said Harry.

'I could eat a whole chicken,' I said. 'But a leg would be nice.'

Soon we were sitting at the table with Hades patrolling underneath, spitting with fury that we had shut him out of the kitchen where he had nefarious plans for the carcass. The combined smell and taste of the roast chicken lifted my spirits and soon I could enjoy the company of my favourite people and join in the banter. Not much remained after we had all eaten seconds and fed morsels to Hades. Soon we were all relaxing on the sofa and exchanging information on the case.

After I had told them all about the goings on at Tarton, Mouse opened his laptop and opened some tabs in his browser. I marvelled at the speed of his fingers on the keyboard.

'Here we are,' he said. 'Safe Haven historical archive.'

'Um, is that legal?' said Harry.

'I didn't have to hack the site to find this, so either their security is rubbish or I'm just lucky. Anyway, I searched the records for mentions of the Sheldons. The oldest case I found is the record of Roger Sheldon's insurance pay out. I don't know much about insurance, but there's definitely something funny about this file.'

'What do mean?' I said.

'Well, Roger Sheldon died of a heart attack, in flagrante, as it happens. The autopsy results didn't leave any doubt of the cause. But Safe Haven requested blood tests for drugs and poisons, and when they came back negative, demanded they be retested to make sure. Then they asked Lydia Sheldon for her marriage certificate and other papers. This caused a total delay of at least three months in the payout of the insurance.'

'She told us the truth then. The insurance company delayed payment of her husband's insurance policy for three months for no good reason.'

'But why would they do that?' said Harry.

'I don't know, but she lost the house, because she couldn't make the mortgage payments,' I said

'But how come they had a mortgage? Didn't her family own the house for hundreds of years?' he said.

'Supposedly. It doesn't make sense. What about the subsidence claim?' I said.

'The new owners of Tarton Manor House, the Tippings, pretended an oak tree to the west of the house had caused subsidence, and they used it as an excuse to cut it down. Safe Haven sent an assessor out to check the damage and sign the reports. Dermot told me the tree was too far from the house to cause any damage and they wanted to cut it down to build the conservatory,' said Mouse.

'Do these claims have anything in common?' said Harry.

'Funny you should ask,' said Mouse, tapping the side of his mouse. 'There were three people who started in personal insurance and transferred to buildings insurance over the years. Only one of them is a qualified assessor.'

'What's his name?' I said.

'Ray Colthard.'

'You're kidding.'

'No.'

'But he sat beside me at the wedding.'

'I know. What on earth was he doing there? Did he know George?' said Harry.

'I don't think so. But I'll ask him to be sure.'

'That leaves Sharon. Maybe Theresa will know why Sharon invited him.'

'What if nobody invited him?' I said.

'What do you mean?'

'He could have easily come in and put an extra chair at the odds and sods table. No one would have noticed.'

'But why would he come? If he worked for the Tippings, he would have zero interest in killing Sharon with a flower pot. They wanted to keep the hotel open, not close it.'

'Maybe he was spying? Or putting the squeeze on someone.'

'On who?'

'Well, this may be stretching it a little, but it's possible the Tippings were being blackmailed by someone who knew how precarious their situation was with the insurance company. Someone who knew what they had done to own and invest in it.'

'Ray Colthard?' said Harry.

'Exactly.'

'Who would be his natural contact in the hotel?' said Mouse.

'The manager. Tim Boulting. He's as creepy as hell,' I said. 'I saw him hanging around in the passageway during the wedding,' I said. 'I wonder if he had a rendezvous with Colthard.'

'Do you remember how Boulting gloated about the murder?' said Harry. 'He even suggested the hotel could make money out of running murder weekends as a result.'

I had a sudden flash of memory.

'He didn't want us to search the changing rooms either. Maybe he loosened the pot and then hid the chisel in the men's changing room. He may have thrown it out of the window, intending to collect it outside where no one would notice, instead of carrying it through the hotel. I imagine the wedding being arranged at short notice overwhelmed him and he forgot to go up and remove it before then.'

'Do you think he's the one who knocked out Dermot?' said Mouse.

'Good call,' said Harry.

'If he noticed Dermot finding the chisel, I imagine he panicked. It's likely Boulting's DNA got left on the handle.'

'Is there any CCTV at the hotel?' said Mouse. 'The porter is often a good source of gossip. Maybe we could ask him some questions.'

I gasped.

'What?' said Harry.

'Antrim and I had mud all over our shoes after searching the rose bed and Boulting asked us to remove them and leave them for the porter to polish. When we collected them, I told the porter he had cleaned my shoes so well, I'd like to bring all my shoes for him to do. He replied that Mr Boulting had made the same comment.'

'So?'

'I assumed Boulting was talking about my shoes. What if the porter cleaned Boulting's shoes for the same reason he did ours?'

'Mud from the rose bed?' said Mouse.

'Exactly.'

'Who do we speak to first?' said Harry.

'If what we think is correct, we should tell D.I. Antrim first and let them question the porter.'

'But this is our clue,' said Mouse.

'He'll tell me the result. We have to trust him. Whether we like or not, this case is a joint effort now.'

Chapter 25

The next morning, I woke early and lay in the dark bedroom trying to not disturb Harry, whose eyelids were flickering in deep REM sleep. I knew he had nightmares sometimes, but he always denied it. I don't think anyone comes out of active service undamaged. He hadn't talked about Nick for a while, but I guessed knowing where Nick lived gave Harry sufficient comfort for the time being. My phone vibrated on the side table and I picked it up to squint at the screen. I didn't recognise the number, but the message made it plain who sent it. I pressed the call back button.

'Theresa? It's Tanya.'

'Hi there. I wondered if you still wanted to talk to me about Sharon. I'll be at the storage lockers this morning if you fancy a chat.'

'The ones behind Sainsbury's?'

'Yes. I've got a big white van.'

'Would you like me to bring us a flask of tea?'

'Yes please.'

'Of course. What time would suit you?'

'Ten? That will give me an hour to sort some stuff out first. We've got one of the half-size shipping containers beside the car park.'

'I'll meet you there.'

I hung up and scrolled through the latest news, regretting it instantly. May you live in interesting times is an ironic blessing for a reason. Harry grunted and turned over to face me.

'Don't you ever sleep?'

'I've nearly had eight hours. Anyway, Theresa sent me a text. She wants to meet up this morning.'

'Are you sure that's a good idea?'

'It can't hurt. She's the only one who knew about Sharon's business.'

'Do you still think the Hurleys could have something to do with her death? The information Mouse dug up seems to give a pretty strong indication that Boulting loosened the flower pot.'

'Agreed. But did he shove it off the balcony or was it someone else?'

'Ah the sixty-four-thousand-dollar question.'

I pecked him on the cheek and rolled out of bed. The floor felt icy under my bare feet and I almost jumped back in again. The thought of snuggling with Harry tempted me greatly. I put on my slippers and dressing gown and wandered to the bathroom for a shower. The hot water felt wonderful and I luxuriated in a good clean with my loofah. When I emerged, I found a text from Ghita telling me to call Roz. I towelled myself dry at top speed and threw on my clothes before I got cold again. Then I crept downstairs trying to let the men sleep a little longer.

'Roz? It's me. How's Dermot?'

'He's awake, thank goodness. Someone hit him with a spade. The doctor said he must have a thick skull to have survived. He'll have to stay in hospital for a few days for monitoring, but all being well, they'll release him then.'

'Thank goodness. I have been worried sick.'

'I managed to speak to him for a minute. He told me to tell you he found a chisel in the rose bed under the men's changing room window.'

'You told me that yesterday. I bet it had DNA on it too. No wonder somebody wanted it back.'

'How did it go with Antrim? He's a dark horse, isn't he? I reckon he fancies you.'

'No, he doesn't. It's strictly business. He wants to find the murderer as much as I do. Anyway, the clues seem to be pointing to an accident right now, or an opportunistic murder. Nothing premeditated.'

'Whose aim is that good anyway? The pot could have just as easily fallen to the floor without hitting anyone.'

'I'm meeting Theresa Hurley this morning.'

'Sharon's sister? Isn't she anti the police?'

'I'm not the police, or has it escaped your notice? Anyway, I want to get some information about their business. I can't help feeling the Hurleys are mixed up in this somehow. Anyway, I've got to go now. Will you keep me in the loop about Dermot. Mouse would like to visit him later if it's possible.'

'Be careful.'

I texted D.I. Antrim to let him know I would be meeting Theresa at the storage depot. He didn't answer, which I presumed meant he was driving to the station. I gulped down a cup of tea and poured the rest of the pot into a flask. Then I ate a piece of toast with lemon curd to tide me over. I tidied the kitchen and fed Hades to make the most of the time before meeting Theresa. He rubbed himself against my legs before remembering he didn't like me. I grinned at him and he stalked off.

I put the tea in my satchel with a couple of mugs and went out to the car which had a layer of snow on the windshield. The windscreen wipers soon cleared it off and I set out on roads already cleared by the weak morning sunshine. The roads were relatively free of traffic since the rush hour had long finished and I made good time to the storage depot. I parked my car and headed for the enclosure containing the shipping containers. A security man stopped me at the gate and I had to text Theresa to come and let me in. She arrived lugging two bags for life from Tesco containing box folders. I could tell how heavy they were by the way her arms were straining.

'There's no need to come in,' she said, putting up a hand. 'We can look at these in the back of the white van.'

Her hand had white marks on them where the heavy bag had cut into her palm. I marvelled at her strength as I staggered under the weight of the one bag that I took one from her. We carried them over to the back of the van which opened to reveal a basic office set up

'Wow, this is amazing,' I said. 'A mobile office.'

'Sharon came up with the idea. It's a lot cheaper than renting.'

Theresa had less makeup on than usual and her resemblance to Sharon gave me a start. She had been right to accuse me of being callous. How would I have felt if it were Helen who had been killed instead of Sharon? She peered down the road as if expecting someone, but perhaps making sure Fintan wasn't on his way. I patted the file boxes.

'Are these the accounts?'

'They're all the company papers, including communications, invoices and receipts.'

'Why haven't you entered the data into an accounting software?'

'I'm doing a course at the Tech; first level business accounting. We were doing everything on paper until I graduated. Anyway, I thought you might be able to spot any problems in the original documents.'

'What sort of problems?'

She didn't answer.

'How about that cup of tea then? I'm gasping. I've been on a detox this week and I've had a headache for four days straight.'

'Rather you than me. Does Fintan go on these health kicks with you?'

She spluttered with laughter.

'His idea of detox is to cut out mushy peas. He thinks he's a hard man.'

While I poured the tea, my cell phone pinged at me. I glanced at the screen to see that Flo had sent me a message telling me they had Fintan Hurley on CCTV using Sharon's credit card and they were bringing him in for a chat. I froze. How long before he contacted Theresa? She might think I agreed to this meeting in order to get information for the police. I decided to risk it.

'Did he have a lot to do with the business? Or did you keep it between sisters?'

'We set it up together without George or Fintan. George stayed well out of it, to give him his due, but Fintan kept trying to interfere. He's not much of a business man to tell you the truth. The clients found him intimidating so we only used him in an emergency.'

'Probably for the best.'

A well-dressed man got out of a car and approached the van. He greeted Theresa who smiled at him and asked him what he wanted. He shuffled and looked at his feet.

'I know you've had troubles. I hope you'll accept my condolences for the loss of your sister. A terrible accident. It's just that I haven't been paid for your order. My wife's up in arms. She needs the money for our next batch of stock.'

'I sent Fintan to pay you with cash a couple of weeks ago, before the wedding. Are you saying he didn't give you the money?'

'He told us we would have to wait for our money, because you were expecting a payment from a client.'

Theresa's jaw worked and I could see she had to fight to retain her self-control.

'I'm really sorry about that. He must have got confused. Can I give you half now, and I'll bring the rest around later?'

'I suppose half is better than nothing,' he said.

Theresa fished around in her voluminous handbag and pulled out a fat wallet. She removed all the notes from the pocket in it and counted them into the man's hand. Then she wrote a receipt on a piece of paper and asked him to sign it.

'More for my benefit than yours,' she said. 'I'd forget my head if it wasn't screwed on tight.'

The man hesitated. I could almost hear the cogs whirring in his head.

'Just so you know,' he said. 'Fintan has been telling the other suppliers, they'll be dealing with him from now on.'

The man walked off, recounting the money Theresa had given him. She sighed and her head dropped.

'So now you know why we didn't work with Fintan. He's always been too far from the beaten track for Sharon. I tolerate him, but not for much longer.'

'And Sharon?'

'She thought he might be planning to steal our business. She may even have suspected me of cooperating which is worse. Take the accounts away with you and have a look. Let me know if you can spot anything that might be a motive for murder. Maybe one of the suppliers had a grudge.'

I wanted to stay and ask more questions, especially about Fintan, but I didn't feel like pushing my luck. After thanking her, I put the box files in the boot of my car and set off for the Grotty Hovel.

Chapter 26

I found Mouse and Harry still at home having a coffee in the sitting room and got Harry's help to carry the box files in from the car. He enjoyed showing off his strength and I loved to see him flex his biceps when asked to carry something. He called it 'man's work', but only as a joke. I got a kick out of seeing the ease with which he moved heavy objects like they were feathers. I suppose we were stereotypical man and woman in that way, but mostly we had a great partnership. I still hadn't agreed to marry him, but he didn't push me to decide. I rubbed his bald head and gave him a smoochy kiss which made us both pink in the cheeks.

'Get a room,' said Mouse, covering his eyes and pretending to faint on the sofa. 'What are the stone age files for?'

'They're from Sharon's business. Theresa asked me to check them for fraud.'

'Does she think Sharon fiddled the books?' said Harry.

'No. It's Fintan she's worried about, and for good reason, he's just been taken in for questioning about using Sharon's credit card to take out money from the bank.'

'Does Theresa know?' said Mouse.

'I got a text from Flo at the storage depot, but I chickened out of telling Theresa. She'll find out soon enough. I thought she wouldn't give me the accounts and I want to be able to check them as soon as possible.'

'So, me then?' said Mouse.

'Can you? I'll help.'

'And what about me?' said Harry.

'I'd like you to open the shop if you're not busy,' I said. 'There are a couple of pieces of furniture down the back of the shop which need a little TLC if you've got the inclination.'

'I quite fancy a bit of that. Will you be in later?'

'I hope so. We only need to find a couple of examples to photocopy on the printer and I'll give them to D.I. Antrim for his case.'

After Harry had left for Second Home, Mouse and I sat at the table and poured over the accounts. Theresa had entered all the invoices and payments into an old-fashioned ledger, so matching the paper invoices and receipts with the ledger did not present a challenge. I noticed that one or two of the invoice amounts had been altered and increased. The corresponding receipts were for the original amount, but the signatures were illegible. I got Mouse to ring one of the suppliers and pretend he had spilled coffee on an invoice. He asked them to tell him the correct figure so he could note it down. I watched his eyes widen as they read the original to him. He thanked them and put down the phone.

'It's the first figure,' he said. 'Someone has increased the invoice amount and then written a receipt for the original figure.'

'I saw Theresa and Sharon both pay cash to suppliers. I bet they were avoiding tax. And if Fintan paid the suppliers sometimes, it looks like he skimmed an extra few percent off the top for himself.'

'Fintan changed the invoices?'

'Looks like it.'

'Do you think Sharon found out?'

'I'm beginning to think she did. Maybe that's why she sounded unsure on her wedding day. She trusted George more than the Hurleys.'

My phone pinged at me. I had received a text from Flo asking me to come to the station to talk to D.I. Antrim. George had gone back to work there, as he had been cleared of suspicion, but conflict of interests meant he couldn't be involved in the case. I wondered how he could cope with being in the station listening to people discussing the possible murder of his wife on their wedding day.

'I've got to go,' I said. 'Can you make a list of the dodgy invoices and call the suppliers to check the real amounts? I'm going to make a copy of the one we already checked and take it with me to show D.I. Antrim.'

Mouse gave me a thumbs up. He already had his head down over the boxes and his total concentration made him mute. He didn't like to speak while he researched. I kissed the top of his head and wrinkled my nose at Hades who peeped out of his laundry basket to see where I was going.

I decided to walk along the promenade, taking with me a supply of stale bread for a quick pit stop in the wind shelter. A strong westerly gale blew along the coast making the waves break sideways against the pebble banks. My hair streamed in front of my face and strands crept into my mouth, so I pulled it into a bun under my beanie. The wind shelter smelled of urine, a not infrequent occurrence, but I tried to block it out. The next rain storm would wash the odour away. I sat on the bench at the pier-end of the shelter, completely sheltered from the wind and assembled my thoughts. Despite the evidence pointing to the Boulting-Coulthard relationship, Fintan had now assumed the mantel of prime suspect. I couldn't figure out how he managed to get to Theresa in time to come running to the passageway. Surely, she would have noticed if he had dashed to her side?

As I mused, Herbert floated in and landed with a splat on his rubbery feet. He cocked his head to one side and I reached into the bag of bread and threw him some crusts. He gobbled them down, throwing them to the back of his throat as if they were fish. Then I gave him a whole slice of toast which he balanced in his beak before taking off again leaving me wondering. Maybe I would find out some new information at the station. I got to my feet and started off to the station again at a brisk gait, passing the Pavilion Theatre at the entrance to the pier and crossing the road at the Seafood Hut. By the time I got to the station building, the only part of me still cold was my nose which throbbed like Rudolph's. Carol Burns looked up from painting her nails as I came in. A sneer hovered around her mouth, but she dredged up a greeting, if not a smile.

'Good morning. Here again? There's no smoke without fire is there?'

I refused to be drawn, despite the easy target of her ghastly outfit.

'That's a nice blouse. It goes with your eyes.'

A startled expression scampered across her face. I smiled without showing any teeth.

'Thank you. Are you here for Fintan?' she said.

'No, thanks. Oh, you mean to answer questions about him? Yes, I am.'

'He's a wrong un. I could tell from the beginning. His police record rivals the Krays.'

A massive exaggeration, but I let it pass.

'I'm sure D.I. Antrim will find out the truth.'

'He's not half the man George is.'

'Fintan? No, of course not.'

'I meant D.I. Antrim. George is twice the man he is.'

'So you said. I think D.I. Antrim's rather dishy.'

The door opened as I opened my mouth to say that, and who should hear me but the man himself. He hid a smirk. I rolled my eyes. For heaven's sake. As if!

'Are you ready, Ms Bowe? It certainly sounds like it.'

I could have punched him. Carol tittered and waved her newly painted nails in the air like some kind of weird semaphore. I grunted, pink with embarrassment, and he guided me through the door with a light touch in the small of my back. So light, I thought I'd imagined it. We walked past the bank of glass and hardboard partitions with their fluorescent lighting. I looked into one room to see George tapping on his keyboard, his brow furrowed. I couldn't catch his eye before D.I. Antrim whisked me into the interview room. I forgot to take my shoes off and was rewarded by an electric shock when I tried to pull the chair out from under the table. I jumped back and swore.

'Some of us never learn,' said Antrim. 'Take Fintan Hurley for instance. I suppose you heard we have him in the cells.'

''Now where would I have heard that?' I said, feigning innocence and knowing he knew I knew that he knew exactly where.

'CCTV caught him using Sharon's bank card in the ATM. We brought him in for questioning. Does that surprise you?'

'Not really,' I said, handing him the photocopies of the faked invoices. 'He skimmed cash off Sharon's business too.'

'Where did you get these?'

'Theresa Hurley gave them to me.'

'We'll need to get her in for questioning too. Have you remembered anything else about the wedding? Specifically, about the Hurleys?'

'They knew I heard them talking about George. Fintan deliberately drew his finger across his throat... Oh.'

'What?'

'Sharon was behind me. She came to tell me about the gift she had for me. Could he have been signalling her instead of me?'

'Why would he want her dead?'

'I heard a supplier tell Theresa that Fintan told them they'd be dealing with him from now on.'

'What date was this?'

'I don't know.'

'If it was before the wedding, this could be premeditation.'

'But he didn't loosen the pot. Or knock Dermot out.'

'We don't know that. I heard he was hanging around at Tarton Manor House before the wedding. We'll need to check up on it.'

'Do you need me to do anything?'

'Stay out of it for now. We'll get Theresa Hurley to come in. Unfortunately, we can't hold Fintan much longer, but we can remand him in custody if we get enough evidence.'

Later that evening, a hysterical text landed in my inbox from Theresa Hurley calling me a snitch and a grass. When I didn't answer it, she called me over and over until I put my phone under a cushion. But she kept calling. Finally, I picked it up and held the phone away from my ear while she yelled and screamed.

'Did I lie?' I said, when she paused for breath. 'I thought you wanted to know who killed your sister. I'm sorry if the clues are pointing to your husband, but that's not my fault.'

'You gave them receipts. You betrayed my trust.'

'I don't remember you telling me they were secret. You asked me to find the person who killed your sister, and I'm trying to do that. What if Fintan is the murderer?'

I heard her sobbing furiously at the other end of the line.

'He isn't. I know him. He's no angel, but he wouldn't kill Sharon.'

I remembered thinking the same about George. I still believed it, because I knew him. Didn't Fintan deserve the benefit of the doubt too?

'If he didn't do it, he won't get charged. You may not trust the police, but D.I. Antrim's a straight copper. I get inside information from the station all the time and I've heard good things about him. He's a fair man.'

'But they're stitching him up. Now they're accusing him of knocking out some gardener fellow at Tarton Manor House. He's got an alibi for that, only...'

I heard her sigh. I finished the sentence in my head for her. *Only he was doing something nefarious and he doesn't want to tell the police.*

'Have they charged him with anything?'

'No. They wanted me to report him for using Sharon's card without permission, as I'm her heir, but I refused.'

'They'll have to release him tomorrow if they can't charge him. Be patient. I'm still working on a few things concerning the ownership of the hotel. I promise to get to the bottom of it. There's a chance someone who works there had a motive to kill, but his plan backfired and the wrong person died.'

She sniffed loudly.

'Someone killed her by mistake?'

'Maybe. I promise we're all doing our best to find out who killed your sister, and I know you're having a tough time, but you've got to be patient.'

'It's easy for you to say. What if it was your sister lying dead outside the toilets?'

'I'd be devastated. Like you are. I'm so sorry.'

But she had hung up. I flopped back on the sofa, my jaw clenched in frustration.

'Tough call,' said Harry. 'What can I do to help?'

'Can you come with me to interview Ray Colthard?'

'Sure. Maybe Mouse can find out where he works and we'll pay him a visit.'

'Can we go tomorrow?'

'Not possible. We've got a clearance.'

'Seriously?'

'In one of the blocks along the road to Lancing. It sounds like a classic.'

I gave him a hug and stayed wrapped around him on the sofa. I would have purred if I knew how. A field trip always made me feel better.

Chapter 27

The apartment block sat on the shore between Seacastle and Lancing, sheltered from the stiff breeze by its sister blocks, identical to all extents and purposes. We parked outside in a vacant space opposite the front door. I stared up at the wind battered façade with Harry.

'Are you sure this is the correct one?' I said. 'I once saw a film in a Russian colleague's flat on New Year's Eve about a drunk guy who found himself at the wrong flat in identical blocks in a different city and let himself in.'

Harry raised an eyebrow.

'And what were you doing with him in his flat?'

'Actually, my colleague was a she, is a she. Natasha Golova; I worked with her on *Uncovering the Truth*. I always suspected she might have been a spy, moonlighting on the programme for extra cash.'

'Is she still in London?'

'I'm not sure. The Cold War had finished, but now it seems to be returning. Who knows if she's still an asset? Or ever was?'

'What happened in the film?'

'The drunk guy falls in love with the woman who owns the flat.'

'And they live happily ever after?'

'Maybe. I don't speak Russian, so I couldn't be sure.'

'You watched the film without subtitles?'

'We had lots of champagne. I didn't really notice. Apparently, it's a tradition in Russia to watch this film on New Year's Eve.'

'We used to watch Monty Python and the Holy Grail.'

'I like Galaxy Quest now. You'll have to watch that if you come to the Grotty Hovel for New Year's Eve.'

'I'm game if you are. Let's go up. The flat is on the fifth floor.'

We called the lift and swayed on our feet as it juddered its way up.

The door to the flat had a single lock which needed to be jiggled before it would give. The door swung open as Harry managed to free the latch and I walked into a world stuck in a time warp. The flat screamed vintage at me. My hand flew to my mouth as I registered the treasures contained within. Some of the furniture had come from Heals or Habitat in the 1960s but a lot of the pieces were Italian. I had a weird feeling I would know the answer, but I asked anyway.

'What were the owners called?'

'Bonetti, I think.'

Sadness almost overwhelmed me as I realised that we were in the flat of the owners of the Italian café almost opposite Second Home. Rohan and Kieron had taken over the empty restaurant when the Bonettis has retired and returned to Italy. I couldn't believe the Bonettis had left so many of their treasures behind. Perhaps their children had no interest in adding them to their households. I ran my hand along the top of the one remaining chair and gazed around. A cocktail cabinet with red Bakelite handles on its doors stood empty against the back wall. The veneer had lifted slightly in one corner, but could easily be reattached with no sign of damage. I wondered if it had been a wedding present, or an early purchase, now abandoned in an empty flat. A shelf above the electric fireplace held a collection of Italian vases. I spied a pair of Giulianelli sgraffito ceramic pieces with angel fish on them. I examined them closely. They were in mint condition except for some water staining inside which could probably be removed.

The rest of the sitting room had almost been cleared of furnishings. A clean square of carpet marked the spot where a cupboard had been removed. Somebody had converted a turquoise Fratelli Fanciullacci leaf vase into a table lamp by drilling a hole at the bottom for the wire, and it now sat on the floor instead of the cupboard. A Mancioli ceramic tray decorated with colourful condiment containers lay on the centre on the coffee table. A couple of pistachio nuts still in their shells sat in one compartment, witnesses to their owner's last snack. I bent down to inspect the coffee table which had four slim conical legs forming V-shaped struts at either end of the oblong table top. I removed the tray and tipped the table over. A gasp escaped me as I read the sticker on the bottom. Guglielmo Ulrich.

'Anything good?' said Harry.

'It's great,' I said. 'Grace will want this. I think our luck has turned. I can't understand why the Bonettis didn't take all this with them.'

'Perhaps they took all the best pieces already? There's no way of knowing how full the flat was before they moved.'

'That's true. I guess its only stuff in the end.'

We packed the ceramics in bubble wrap and stored them in boxes. Then we made several trips in the scary lift to take everything downstairs to the van. We locked up the flat and pushed the keys through the letter box. I felt torn between joy and sadness at our haul. Clearance work could push my pathos button every time. We drove back to the shop and started to unpack our treasures. I pondered giving the angel fish vases to Rohan and

Kieron for Surfusion, but instead I put them in the window to see if I could sell them first. I loved Rohan, but sometimes Kieron could be a little abrasive. Even Ghita found him a little difficult compared to Rohan.

Mouse and Roz helped us to unwrap our new finds and wipe the ceramics clean in a bucket of hot soapy water. We went upstairs to enter the haul into my log book. I kept a paper one as well as the one on Mouse's iPad. Everything in the shop had been registered and priced in the log, along with provenance and Harry's cut. We kept our finances strictly separate despite practically living together. I preferred it that way, but I don't think Harry noticed one way or another. Mouse made us a big pot of tea and we all sat in contemplation of our new finds as darkness fell outside.

My phone rang and I grabbed it thinking Helen had arrived back from visiting Olivia at university.

'Hello?'

'Tanya. It's Flo. Something terrible has happened.'

'Is someone hurt?'

'Dead. A neighbour found Fintan Hurley lifeless in his flat. An ambulance took him to the hospital, but they couldn't revive him.'

I gasped. Poor Theresa.

'What on earth happened to him?'

'A blow to the head. I can't tell you anymore yet. It may be accidental. SOCO think it may be a robbery gone wrong.'

'That's terrible.'

'There's more. They found something in his pocket. A brooch wrapped in red tissue paper. There are traces of blood on the brooch.'

'What about the tissue paper?'

'I don't know yet. That's all they told me. I've got to go now.'

'Thanks Flo. You're a treasure. Keep me posted.'

I dropped the phone into my bag and looked around at my friends who had various expressions of shock and concern on their faces.

'Who's dead?' said Roz.

'Fintan Hurley.'

'Was he murdered?' said Mouse.

'They don't know yet. It may have been an attempted burglary which turned fatal.'

'Why were you asking about tissue paper?' said Harry.

'They found a brooch in Fintan's pocket, wrapped in red tissue paper.'

'Didn't Sharon buy you a brooch in Grace's shop to give to you at the wedding?' said Roz.

'She did. D.I. Antrim and I found the note and some red tissue paper stuffed down the side of the couch in the women's changing room at Tarton Manor House.'

'He killed her and stole the brooch?' said Mouse. 'Her brother-in-law? But why would he do that?'

'What was he doing in the women's changing room? And why would he stuff only half of the tissue paper down the couch?' said Harry.

'This doesn't sound right,' said Mouse. 'Why did he kill her?'

'I'm not sure. He may have wanted to take over her business.'

'Why steal the brooch,' said Harry.

'It may have been valuable. But you're right. Who would risk stealing the brooch to sell on? It's Art Deco. Easy to recognise. Hard to fence.'

'Poor Theresa,' said Mouse. 'First her sister and now her husband.'

We all sighed. I knew I'd have to talk to her again, not a prospect I looked forward to.

'If somebody killed Fintan in a robbery, why didn't they steal the brooch?' said Roz.

Chapter 28

It didn't take long for forensics to get the results back from the blood found on the brooch in Fintan's pocket. It matched exactly with the splatter on the tissue paper D.I. Antrim and I found stuffed down the side of the couch. The blood belonged to Sharon Walsh. The case appeared to be sewn up in some respects, but I couldn't get my head around it. Just because Fintan had Sharon's brooch in his pocket did not mean he had dropped the gargoyle flower pot onto her head. And what man would hide in the women's changing room instead of making himself scarce through the doors into the main body of the hotel?

And who had killed Fintan Hurley? The police were going through the motions investigating the burglary, but Flo told me their attitude read as good riddance to bad rubbish as far as Fintan was concerned. I could sympathise with them, but it felt like they had been handed their murder suspect tied up with red tissue paper and a bow. I tried to talk to George, but he refused to engage with me.

'You're not a detective, Tan. There are things you don't understand. You need to drop your investigation.'

'But I've still got questions about Fintan's death. What sort of burglar doesn't steal a valuable brooch?'

'Maybe they were disturbed and ran away. Who knows? Someone had ransacked the drawers. We think

Fintan found a person in his flat and they hit him too hard by mistake.'

'But what about the tissue paper?'

'What tissue paper? You're the only one who's still asking questions. I just want to move on from the tragedy and get my station back from Antrim. Can't you understand that?'

I tried. I reasoned with myself as I decorated the shop window for Christmas, and while I prepared supper in the kitchen at the Grotty Hovel. The doubts kept resurfacing no matter how often I tamped them down, like a game of whack-a-mole. I wanted to call Theresa to give her my condolences, but I lacked the courage to face the barrage of recriminations and vitriol I might receive. Fintan's funeral would take place in Liverpool and I could think of nowhere I would be less welcome. Theresa's suffering didn't bear thinking about.

Looking for certainty, I rang Flo.

'I suppose you're wanting the results of the autopsy,' she said. 'They won't tell you anything we didn't already know. Fintan died of a blow to the head, delivered when his back had been turned.'

'He turned his back on the burglar? Does that sound likely unless he knew his killer.'

'Perhaps he did. Fintan Hurley had a load of dodgy friends. It may have been a drug deal that went wrong. Or just greed. SOCO have swabbed the flat, but I don't hold out much hope of a breakthrough. Every criminal in Seacastle must have visited Fintan at one time or another. The trove of fingerprints will be a who's who of the local crime scene.'

D.I. Antrim had no sympathy with my point of view either.

'It's unfortunate, but it happens. Fintan hung out with dodgy companions, any of whom may have suspected him of keeping cash in his flat. He wasn't exactly popular among his peers either. There are dozens of possible suspects.'

'Do you still think the brooch proves that he killed Sharon?'

'Contrary to popular wisdom, we don't follow our gut feelings, although most people have him as a strong suspect. I'm working with the evidence. So far, the information we have points to him as our killer. We need to dot the i's and cross the t's first before we take it to the Crime Prosecution Service.'

I could see their point of view. Fintan looked nailed on for the murder of his sister-in-law. The police had traced the supplier who had reported Fintan's comment about being in charge soon. He had made it just before the wedding. And yet I couldn't escape the feeling we had missed something. I made a visit to the wind shelter to feed Herbert and mutter to myself like a mad old bat. He sidled up to see me and accepted the crusts before leaving again without ceremony as if he didn't want to hear about the case either.

The relatively mild weather had brought people out onto the beach and I watched them stride along, leaning into the wind with their scarves flying behind them. Dogs capered about dragging stalks of seaweed from the latest storm and brushing the sand with the fronds of kelp. I took some deep breaths and tried to expel my troubles and take in the panorama. A couple came into my field of view who seemed familiar. They walked arm in arm with synchronised steps, talking animatedly and laughing. I screwed up my eyes to focus on them and my jaw dropped almost onto the ground. George and Helen. My sister and my ex-husband on a stroll along Seacastle beach, looking for all the world like an established couple. Shaking my head, I looked again. I had not been mistaken. For some reason, I felt embarrassed to have spotted them. I sat back on the bench shrinking against the wall, so they wouldn't notice me.

Too late. I saw them stop and stare at the wind shelter. Helen appeared to pull George's arm and attempt to start towards me. He shook his head and gestured along the beach. She put her hands on her hips. Never a good sign. But he held out. She had finally met her match. Despite myself, I couldn't help a smug smile creeping onto my lips. Her body language as she approached reminded me of a small child caught robbing the biscuit tin. She could hardly look me in the eye. I raised my eyebrows at her and waited for her to speak.

'It's only a walk,' she said.

'Oh. Is that what it is?' I said. 'It looked like a date to me.'

The muscles in her face danced in frustration as she searched for an excuse. Defeated, she sat beside me and took my hand.

'Okay. You caught us. We're seeing each other. Sort of.'

'Sort of?'

'I wanted to ask you, to tell you, but I worried you might be upset. It's all extremely weird right now. George is going through a hard time.'

'A hard time? It's Sharon who's dead.'

'You know what I mean. He found out she never loved him, and he wanted to leave her anyway, until the baby...'

She trailed off. I hadn't the heart to tell her about his plan to return to me. Somehow that phase of both our lives had ended the day Sharon died. All my feelings of hurt and longing around George had faded day by day once I had met Harry. There seemed to be no point in being a dog in the manger about George, especially as Helen and George fitted together like two halves of a coin. He wanted someone who would have dinner on the table when he got home. She couldn't wait to have it ready for him. He loved his shirt with a pinch of starch. Helen loved to iron while watching cozy mysteries on the television. I had no dogs in this particular fight any more. I sighed.

'You should be more discreet. George is not completely off the hook with Antrim yet, and if Antrim sees George hanging out with you, he may feel obliged to investigate your relationship.'

'You're right, of course. It just seems like we've been waiting for this all our lives, somehow. You're not cross with me, are you?'

'Don't be silly. If you and George find happiness together, we'll all be thrilled. You'd be so good for him. It's weird for me though. I need time to get my head around it.'

'I do, but you and George are history now. Maybe if I'd met him first...'

'Maybe,' I said.

I couldn't compute. Harry and I were happy, and I knew I should be pleased for her, but I couldn't help feeling betrayed by both of them for different reasons. We sat there contemplating the vista together. A boy ran by pulling a kite behind him, letting the string spool up into the sky.

'Do you think Fintan killed Sharon?' I said.

'Talk about changing the subject.'

'Do you?'

'Maybe. He might have done it on the spur of the moment when he found the loose pot.'

'What if he knew it was loose before the wedding?'

'We can't ask him anymore. Maybe you should forget it. Everybody is happy now.'

Everyone except me, I thought.

Chapter 29

I kept their secret to myself, one of many things I couldn't talk about. Life moved on without me. I pretended to be Tanya in the present day, but my brain refused to drop the subject of Sharon's murder. A clue had been overlooked, but D.I. Antrim had gone back to Brighton and George had zero interest in pursuing my leads. This did not put me off, but I felt stranded, like a jellyfish on the beach waiting for the tide.

When I could stand it no longer, I walked to the Shanty to have a drink with Ryan and Joy, and gaze out at the sea. Ryan grinned when he saw me duck under the short doorway and enter white-faced from the cold. He prepared me a hot port without being asked and placed it on the table in front of me, lowering his wheelchair so our heads were on the same level.

'What do you think of my new wheels?' he said. 'I've added some new capabilities to it.'

'Amazing. You should audition for Q on the next Bond film.'

He smirked, but he swallowed whatever he had been about to say.

'What brings you here all by yourself?' he said. 'Normally, lone drinkers are looking for a chat with the barman.'

'How did you guess?'

'I'm not only a mechanical genius, I'm also psychic. Is it, by any chance, something to do with Sharon Walsh's murder?'

'Got it in one. Everyone thinks Fintan Hurley did it, but I'm not sure at all. There are unanswered questions. I'm so frustrated, but I don't want to bore everyone with my theories.'

'So, you thought you'd bore me instead?'

Ryan said this with a twinkle in his eye, but I still blushed.

'I suppose you could say that. I'd tell Joy if she were here. Where is she anyway?'

'She had to go to Budapest to see our suppliers.'

I nodded as if I believed him. I had never seen them sell any Bulgarian wine at the Shanty, but maybe they had a side hustle. I preferred to think they were spies, as did the majority of the folk who drank there, but we all stuck to the script.

'Do you mind me picking your brains?'

'That's what I'm here for.'

'The police say a burglar killed Fintan when he discovered them in his flat, but Fintan's body had a valuable brooch in his jacket pocket which Sharon Walsh bought from Grace Wong for me.'

'How did he get his hands on the brooch?'

'The police think he stole it from Sharon when he killed her at the wedding.'

'But you don't?'

'That's the logic, but it doesn't make sense. In theory, Fintan killed her by pushing a flower pot off a balcony. But how did he know it was loose in the first place? The pots had recently been cemented in place. He would have had to make a separate trip to the hotel to loosen the cement. Surely someone would have seen him and come forward by now? Whoever loosened the pot had access to the hotel when nobody was around.'

'Who else had a motive to loosen the pot?'

'Tim Boulting, the manager of the hotel. I think someone called Ray Colthard was blackmailing him. He may have taken matters into his own hands.'

'Do you think he killed Sharon?'

'Maybe, but not on purpose. She may have walked underneath at precisely the wrong moment.'

'Do you have any idea who tried to blackmail Tim Boulting?'

'I think so. It's a long story. Tim Boulting doesn't come out of it smelling of roses either.'

'Maybe you should go back to the beginning of the story and work your way forward. That's what we do.'

I froze. A slip of the tongue? I waited. He tilted his head on one side and looked deep into my eyes. His gaze made me shiver as his white-hot intelligence manifested itself for an instant. He shrugged.

'Me and Joy. When we're working. We go back to where it all started.'

I knew he wasn't talking about the pub. I hardly dared form the next sentence, but I might never get the chance again.

'Is it dangerous?'

'It can be,' he said. 'My legs are a testament to that.'

'What happened?'

He looked away from me, out over the sea, lost in his memories. I thought he wouldn't answer, but he did.

'Somebody got trapped in Montenegro, in a safe house. Their cover was blown and the FSB wanted to capture them before they could leave.'

'But isn't the Cold War over?'

'Not in Serbia. The government supports Vladimir Putin. The FSB can do anything they like over there without fear of interference.'

'Did you go alone?'

'No, Joy came too. We posed as a couple on holiday. We were ordered to extract the agent from the safe house and take him to the airport before the FSB realised we had arrived. A simple operation. Almost risk free. But something went wrong and someone shot at the car as we headed for the border.'

He stopped and swallowed a couple of times.

'I'm so sorry.'

'Water under the bridge now.'

'But you're both still working?'

'You noticed?' said Ryan, laughing.

'I suspected.'

'I don't need to tell you—'

'My lips are sealed.'

'It's just in case something happens to us. I want someone to be curious, so we don't disappear without trace. You don't mind?'

'It's an honour. Harry's ex-army and he's got friends. If anything ever happens, we'll be curious.'

'Mum's the word until then.'

'I swear never to tell anyone. I'll forget this conversation right now.'

He nodded and rubbed his chin.

'You still need to discover who killed Sharon Walsh. She wouldn't have won any popularity contests, but she deserves that much. You should find that Ray Colthard guy you mentioned.'

'But I don't have any proof yet.'

'Is there any law against asking questions?' said Ryan.

'No, but he doesn't have to answer me either.'

'What have you got to lose? Drink up and I'll make you another.'

I watched him motor off to the bar and sipped my drink. The hot liquid hit my stomach and I could feel my cheeks radiating heat. The news about their real occupation was hardly a revelation, but I felt proud Ryan had taken me into his confidence. I compartmentalised the new information and locked the door in my mind. I could be super discreet when it came to other people's secrets.

On the other hand, I had no intention of letting someone get away with murder. Somebody at Safe Haven had created a monster by getting Ray Colthard fired, but was he capable of murder? And what about Tim Boulting? He had been belittled and blackmailed by Colthard. Maybe he had snapped and tried to eliminate the source of his misery. D.I. Antrim had not warned me off continuing my investigation. He, not George, was still, theoretically, in charge of the case. Ray Colthard should be easy enough to track down, and he had already shown his willingness to engage with me. I couldn't wait to question him.

Chapter 30

Ray Colthard had disappeared. Even Mouse couldn't find him. The manager of the HR office at Safe Haven Insurance claimed he had left a couple of years before.

'Maybe he's using another name,' said Harry. 'He may be nervous that the investigation has uncovered his involvement with Tim Boulting.'

'We need to talk to someone from his team in Safe Haven,' said Mouse. 'A certain Wendy Fuller worked with him for years, according to the records. She's the one person who's likely to know where he is.'

'But how will we persuade her to talk to us? She isn't under any obligation to tell us anything, and she may be complicit in his schemes.'

'We can tell her that we'll keep quiet if she rats him out,' said Harry.

'Okay, Bugsy Malone. Less of the drama,' I said. 'But it makes sense. She tells us where to find him, and we don't tell him she let us know.'

'She lives at 44 Shore Lane,' said Mouse.

Harry and I drove over to Wendy Fuller's house that evening. We agreed that telling her the truth would be less complicated than coming up with an elaborate ruse for getting Ray's whereabouts from her.

'With any luck, she'll spill the beans without any persuasion,' said Harry.

I rolled my eyes. He'd been reading too much Raymond Chandler, and picked up the hardboiled detective speak popular in the 1950s pulp fiction. I found it quite endearing, but I hoped it was only a phase. He had started to referring to me as his broad too. Honestly, I should never have persuaded him to join me in my investigations.

Wendy Fuller lived on an estate in Shoreham in a neat two-up-two-down with a converted garage. Her husband opened the front door. A large man with a tight t-shirt over his enormous tummy, his blank expression did not change when he saw us.

'We vote Labour,' he said, and went to shut the door again.

'Can we speak to your wife,' I said. 'It's important.'

'She votes Labour too,' he said.

'We're not canvassing for votes. We're looking for a long lost relative,' said Harry.

I had to hand it to him. We had not discussed this approach, but it seemed to work instantly. The man's brow wrinkled.

'Like Davina?'

'Exactly,' I said. 'It won't take long.'

I stepped forward expecting to be let in.

'Wait here,' he said, and shut the door in my face.

'Where did you come up with that idea?' I said.

'Nick's been on my mind again.'

'Don't leave it too long. If something happens to either of you, it will be too late to put it right.'

The door swung open again and the man appeared with Wendy Fuller. He stood close behind her, his hand on her shoulder.

'Hello Wendy,' I said. 'We're looking for a man you used to work with.'

She blinked, but she didn't say anything.

'At Safe Haven,' said Harry.

Her eyes widened.

'Safe Haven?'

'Yes,' I said. 'Our records show you worked together in personal insurance before moving to property at almost the same time.'

Her husband's fingers whitened as he tightened his grip on her shoulder.

'We did?' she said.

''A man called Ray Colthard.'

'That bastard,' said her husband. 'There's no way we're helping him find his lost family.'

'We only need his address, and we'll be out of your hair,' said Harry.

'It can't hurt,' said Wendy. 'That was all a long time ago.'

Her husband's face contorted in fury.

'No, it wasn't. How can you defend that scum? He almost got you fired.'

She shrugged, but his hand stayed clamped to her shoulder.

'Please,' I said. 'He may not be a savoury character, but it's hardly his family's fault.'

Wendy glanced at her husband.

'He uses the name Brian Tipping.'

Her husband pulled her inside.

'Go away, and don't come back,' he shouted.

We walked back to the car.

'Isn't that the name of the family who own the hotel?' said Harry.

'It is,' I said. 'I'll text his name to Mouse now.'

'But didn't his parents move to a nursing home?'

'I imagine they were his grandparents.'

'Ah, yes. Probably.'

By the time we got home, Mouse had found Brian Tipping and obtained an address for him. To my surprise, he seemed reluctant to tell us about it. He made a face at me which I couldn't interpret.

'What's up, rodent boy?' said Harry. 'Usually, you can't wait to tell us all about it.'

'He lives in Harbertonford,' said Mouse.

'You're kidding,' said Harry.

'I don't kid about stuff like this.'

'I don't understand,' I said.

'Nick lives just outside Harbertonford,' said Harry.

'Wow, that's a stunning coincidence,' I said. 'Maybe it's a sign.'

'You should go there,' said Mouse. 'Ray Colthard is the key to the happenings at Tarton Manor House.'

Harry sighed.

'I can't. I'm not ready.'

'We don't have to go and see Nick,' I said. 'You can decide while we're down there.'

'What if we bump into him?'

'Would that be the end of the world?' I said. 'Maybe it would be easier if I'm there with you?'

'I'll think about it,' said Harry, taking the keys to his van and heading for the door.

'Where are you going?' I said.

'Home.'

'But you live here,' said Mouse.

'I need space to think.'

'We'll see you tomorrow then,' I said.

He didn't answer, just nodded and let himself out.

'I'm sorry,' said Mouse.

'Oh, heavens, don't be. It's hardly your fault. I actually told him today that he ought to do something about Nick.'

'Really? That makes me feel a lot better.'

'What did you find out about Colthard. Or should we call him Tipping?'

'He's the nephew of the owners of the hotel. His father is Delia Tipping's younger brother. He did business studies at the South Devon college before starting work at Safe Haven.'

'I wonder did the Tippings set that up? I mean, did he know he would be running a scam to steal Tarton Manor House.'

'Perhaps, he didn't at first, but going by the dates, he must have found out soon enough. Lydia Sheldon's husband died in 1992, the same year he started working there,' said Mouse.

'When did he leave?'

'2015.'

'More than twenty years in the same company. He must have been good at his job, even if he did use it to swindle Lydia Sheldon out of her home.'

'He found time to qualify as an assessor at one stage. That proved useful when his uncle needed to cut down the oak tree.'

'Do you think his family forced him to do this?' said Mouse

'The man I met seemed pretty sure of himself. It's a complete mystery.'

'But we've found him now. Whatever his motives, he can't keep them hidden from us. Do you think Harry will come to Harbertonford?'

'I don't know, sweetheart. He's been struggling to decide about Nick for months. Maybe this will persuade him to reach out.'

'Look what happened with you and Helen. Nothing can come between you now,' he said.

I felt like laughing.

'Almost nothing.'

Chapter 31

Harry turned up with fresh croissants from the bakery early the next morning, filling the house with their delicious buttery aroma which competed with that of the coffee for favourite smell. He didn't say anything about Nick, but he went upstairs and filled a daypack so I knew he would be coming with us. Mouse, who always wore his heart on his sleeve, gave Harry a big hug which made me feel tearful. We were all affected by the tumultuous goings on around us and prone to over react as a result. Hades had no sympathy for our maudlin emotions and yowled loudly about his missing breakfast.

'Can we take him to Devon with us?' said Mouse.

'Don't be silly,' I said. 'He'll run away and join the navy. I'll get Roz to come and feed him.'

We ate breakfast and made a picnic before loading everything into my Mini. I had filled her tank and checked the oil while Mouse and Harry made the picnic, so we were ready to go. We got into the car and then Harry had to get out again as Mouse ran back indoors to pick up all his chargers.

'I was hoping for an electronic free trip,' said Harry.

'We won't get far without the GPS in Devon,' said Mouse. 'There are a million back roads.'

'Maybe we should bring a paper map, just in case,' I said.

'What a quaint suggestion,' said Mouse, who jumped into the back seat with a handful of chargers and wires. Harry, who had been patiently standing outside in the drizzle, got back into the Mini again, putting on his seat belt.

'How long will it take us to get there?' he said.

'About four hours,' I said. 'If we don't stop on the way. We should be there before lunch time. With any luck, we can interview Colthard before lunch and then go and have a picnic.'

'It's seven degrees centigrade outside,' said Mouse. 'Maybe we could eat inside.'

I sighed.

'Why don't you find us a nice pub then?'

The traffic had not yet built up, and in no time at all we were heading for Southampton. Mouse's head did not lift from his iPad for the first hour as he surfed the net and learned all about the nooks and crannies of Devon. Then he emitted a grunt of surprise.

'Guess what?'

'Your battery ran out?' said Harry.

'No, I found something brilliant.'

'What's that, sweetheart?'

'Agatha Christie's house, Greenway, is really close by. We can cross the river on a small boat and visit it. We can stay there too, but it's far too expensive'

'Oh, my goodness. I had no idea. Do you mind, Harry?'

'Mind? Why would I mind? She's the next author on my list now I've read every Raymond Chandler.'

'Fantastic. We'll definitely do that.'

Apart from a quick comfort break for bathrooms and to stretch our legs, we didn't stop on the way to Harberton and arrived at midday on the outskirts of the village. We pulled into the car park of the Church House Inn, a pretty pub beside a medieval church. Cold drizzle had started to fall and we trotted inside to avoid getting wet. The warm interior felt promising and Mouse scouted around for a table. He came back to the bar and elbowed me in the ribs.

'What?' I hissed at him.

He whispered in my ear.

'We need to leave now.'

'Why?'

He looked over at Harry who had been distracted by a social post about the Harberton Croquet and Social Club and whispered again.

'Because there's a bloke over there who's the spitting image of Harry.'

I turned slowly in the direction he had indicated and I spotted a man who could have been Harry's twin, slimmer and slightly grey-haired, but there was no mistaking the resemblance. Panic seized me and I reached over to grab Harry's arm. A shout like a strangled bark from a trapped dog erupted from the man, who had seen us at the bar. Harry spun around and stood transfixed as the man rose, knocking over his chair and walking stiff legged towards us. Mouse looked from one to the other, an expression of genuine fear etched on his features. I pulled him towards me, releasing Harry who faced his brother Nick with resignation.

'Harry? Is that you?'

'I'm afraid so. You can hit me now. Get it over with.'

'You idiot. Why would I hit you?'

'What happened before...'

'You mean what didn't happen. She told me the truth, you know. Ages ago.'

'Why didn't you let me know?'

'I'm not sure. Stupid, I guess. Too proud.'

They stared at each other, like a pair of prize fighters checking out the competition. Mouse whimpered. He always acted tough around his friends, but he had no stomach for violence.

'It's okay, sweetheart,' I said.

Harry turned to reassure him and in the same instant Nick lurched forward and threw his arms around him. They ended up in an awkward sideways embrace and Nick laughed.

'We can't do anything right,' he said, and let go.

'We never could,' said Harry.

I tugged Mouse's arm.

'We're going to find Ray Colthard,' I said. 'We'll be back later.'

'Are you sure?' said Harry, but his body language said he wanted to stay.

'See you later,' said Mouse.

We used the toilets before leaving, trying not to spy on the brothers who had bought pints of beer and were already laughing and joshing each other. Mouse looked with longing at the menu as we left.

'We've got the picnic in the back,' I said. 'Why don't you rescue us a couple of croissants with ham and cheese?'

Chapter 32

We set out from the pub to look for Colthard. I could not think of him as Brian Tipping even though I knew it to be his real name. We ate our croissants as we drove along trying to find his house. Soon we were covered in pastry flakes and completely lost. The GPS did not seem able to pinpoint the address in Harberton. We kept going around in circles. Mouse asked a couple of old ladies if they knew Ray Colthard or Brian Tipping, but was met by shoulder shrugging and shaking of heads. I couldn't understand it. Mouse got more and more frustrated with his iPad. The internet signal had disappeared and he couldn't piggyback on our phones.

'I told you we should have brought paper maps,' I said. 'You shouldn't diss the Stone Age.'

A sulky expression clouded his face.

'We've come all the way here for nothing,' he said. 'I can't believe I got it so wrong.'

'Worse things happen at sea. Where's Dittisham? Harry and Nick need some privacy for an hour or two. Why don't we drive down there and check out the ferry for tomorrow?'

'Okay. Keep going along this road.'

We drove about a mile and a half along a narrow winding road before arriving at a junction.

'What on earth?' said Mouse, pointing to the verge where a signpost almost overgrown with grass read Harbertonford.

'Didn't we just come from Harbertonford?' I said.

'I think it was called Harberton, with no ford.'

'That may explain why we couldn't find Colthard.'

We drove into the village which appeared much larger than Harberton. The signal showed as two bars on my phone.

'Try looking for Colthard's address on the iPad again.'

'It's showing down the next turning to the right.'

'Let's go then.'

Colthard/Tipping's house belonged to a grubby terrace which had seen better days. It did not match up with my idea of the Tipping family or their status. Why had he moved down to Devon to such a scruffy dwelling? Perhaps the police had finally shown an interest in his activities at Safe Haven. I had given D.I. Antrim the information I had on both him and Boulting. Maybe Antrim's inquiries had scared Colthard out of our area and down to Devon. I pulled in to the pavement and switched off the engine.

'Here goes nothing,' I said.

The doorbell didn't work so Mouse thumped on the door with his fist. An exclamation of annoyance floated up the passageway, preceding its owner who looked like he'd just got out of bed. His thin hair stuck out at all angles and he had a sheet crease across one of his shiny cheeks. On closer inspection, he appeared much older than I had imagined before, my age or even a decade more. He had thrown a jumper over his pyjama top, and wore thermal leggings which ended in ancient slippers. I tried to avoid noticing his crotch which bulked in all directions as if he had stuffed a pair of socks down there.

'Oh,' he said, pulling down his jumper. 'It's you. I didn't expect…'

He trailed off. I could almost hear the cogs whirring. He pointed out the sitting room.

'Why don't you take a seat in there? And I'll put on a kettle.'

Mouse and I sat on the ratty old couch in the chilly room until Colthard came back. I noticed he had put on a pair of slightly stained trousers. Anything looked better than the leggings. Despite putting the kettle on, he didn't offer us a drink, but judging by the general standard of hygiene I had seen so far, I would have refused on principle.

He rubbed his stubbly chin.

'Okay. I give up. Why are you here? I presume you don't have romance on your mind, unless it's a threesome?'

He leered at me. I frowned.

'You're in a lot of trouble,' I said. 'The police are looking for you with regards to the double murder at Tarton Manor House.'

He jumped to his feet, but then sat down again, looking confused.

'The double murder? What are you talking about? I heard the bride's death was accidental. I don't know anything about a second death. I haven't got internet down here.'

'So, you haven't heard?' said Mouse. 'Fintan Hurley, the bride's brother-in-law was killed in a break in.'

Colthard blinked.

'And what's that got to do with me. Boulting told me the bride's family were dodgy, but I never imagine it would come to this.'

'What were you doing at the wedding?' I said. 'If you didn't know the bride, or the groom.'

'I was passing by, and I fancied a party,' he said, affecting nonchalance, but his cheeks flamed red in panic.

'Passing by? You'll have to do better than that. I know all about your association with Safe Haven and Tarton Manor House.'

Colthard's eyes widened. He gulped and his large Adam's apple shot up and down his throat. He sniffed.

'What do you know?'

'About Lydia Sheldon's husband and the late payment of his insurance leading to the sale of the hotel to your aunt and uncle? Or the fake subsidence scam?'

'Oh.'

'Were you blackmailing Tim Boulting?' said Mouse. Colthard pouted.

'He deserved it. He's the one who planned the whole thing, and then I got the blame and lost my job.'

'But what about your aunt and uncle?' I said.

'They used me,' he hissed. 'I didn't want to help them, but they made me do it.'

'And how did they do that?' said Mouse.

'I had a gambling problem… I owed some money to some unsavoury people. My uncle said he'd pay it off if I helped them get Tarton Manor House.'

'Why Tim Boulting?'

'He ratted me out to Safe Haven after I outgrew my usefulness. I realised the knowledge I had about his part in the plan could ruin him. So, I started to squeeze him for money.'

'Is that why you were at the hotel on the night of the wedding?'

'Yes. I had asked for another payment for keeping quiet. He was supposed to meet me in the passageway where the murder took place, but he never turned up.'

'I saw him there shortly before the murder,' I said.

'Was that when you went to the bathroom? I followed you out there a couple of minutes later, intending to try and speak to you in private, but you didn't come out. I thought I had missed you, and Boulting, so I went back into the conservatory.'

'Did you see anyone else there?'

'In the passageway? No, but I remember seeing someone going upstairs to the men's changing room out of the corner of my eye.'

'Did you see who it was?'

'No, but they were wearing trousers. I don't recall which colour and that wouldn't be much use, because I'm colourblind anyway.'

'The newspapers are claiming it might have been Fintan who pushed the flower pot over the edge. Unfortunately, I didn't see anyone up there when I came out of the Ladies, but I didn't look up.'

'I remember you coming back to the table and the bride whispering something to you. You left again soon afterwards to go back to the passageway. I decided to cut my losses and go home. I was heading for the front door of the conservatory when I heard the screams.'

'I didn't see you at the wedding after I found the body.'

'I made myself scarce. Nobody missed me. I wasn't supposed to be there at all, remember?'

'Why are you skulking down here?' said Mouse.

'Why do you think I extorted money from Boulting? I owe—'

'Some unsavoury people a lot of money?' I asked.

'Got it in one.'

We drove back to Harberton with mixed feelings. As much as I disliked Colthard, I felt convinced he had nothing to do with Sharon's death. He had been open about his involvement with the Safe Haven scams and his ghastly surroundings almost made me feel sympathy for his self-inflicted exile. Anyway, I couldn't magic up a single motive for him killing Sharon, either on purpose or by mistake. On the other hand, I started to wonder about Tim Boulting and his motives for inviting Colthard to the hotel when a wedding party was going on.

If anyone had privileged access to different areas of the hotel, it must have been Boulting. I had a feeling he knew a lot more about what happened that evening than he had told the police. After all, I saw him right there, in the passageway, around the time of the murder. He had been loitering under the balcony, perhaps waiting for Colthard. He must have seen something relevant and I needed to jog his memory. And why had he knocked out Dermot Murray to get the chisel? If he had. So many questions and they all pointed to his possible involvement in the puzzle.

Beside me, Mouse gazed at the countryside as if he had never seen it before.

'Sometimes I forget,' he said.

'Forget what?'

'How beautiful the world is. I'm so busy looking at my screens all day, I miss stuff.'

'We really need to clear out the back garden. We could put bird feeders and bee homes and plant bushes for wildlife to live in.'

'Wouldn't Hades use the bird feeders as a restaurant?'

'Squirrel a la carte, you mean?'

'He's not fussy.'

'Maybe we should leave it how it is. There's more shelter in there.'

'What about a half and half?'

'I'll speak to Harry. He knows a little about gardening. I haven't a clue. Even my cactus died.'

'Do you think Harry and Nick are getting on well?'

'I hope so. We'll soon find out.'

We pulled into the car park of the Church House Inn and went back inside. The table where Harry and Nick had been sitting stood empty. I looked at Mouse who shrugged.

'The men who were sitting here earlier,' I asked the barman. 'Do you know where they are now?'

'Are you Tanya?' he said.

'Yes.'

'They left you a note.' He reached behind the cash register and pulled out a soggy napkin. He handed it to me sheepishly. 'Sorry, it got wet.'

I straightened it out on the bar and read the message. *We've gone home to get drunk. This may get ugly. Suggest you drive home with Mouse and I'll come on the train. Kisses, Harry.'* Mouse snorted when he read it.

'Honestly, you can't take him anywhere. Do you want to go to Dittisham?' I said.

'We can't. I looked it up when we had internet. Greenway is closed until February.'

I sighed.

'Shall we go home then? I don't feel like staying here.'

'We might as well. Do you want me to drive?'

'I'd rather get home alive.'

Chapter 33

Harry crawled home to the Grotty Hovel two days later, looking much the worse for wear. Physically, he was a wreck, but he had a new lightness of being which I couldn't put my finger on. A weight had been lifted off his shoulders. When I asked him what they had been doing for two days, he said, 'oh, you know, brother stuff'. I didn't probe further, presuming he would tell me when the time was right. Instead, I filled him in on our conversation with Colthard and suggested we go to Tarton Manor House to ask Tim Boulting some difficult questions. I still had no clear idea what Boulting's motive could be for killing Sharon, but I remained convinced that Fintan Hurley did not kill her.

Harry did not need any persuading. We drove to Tarton Manor House the next day and we entered the lobby together. The same porter who I had met with D.I. Antrim came over to us with a big smile. I realised Antrim had not told me the result of any interview with him. Or perhaps he had forgotten to do it?

'Ms Bowe, isn't it? And your um?'

'My partner Harry Fletcher.'

'Mr Fletcher. It's a pleasure to welcome you to Tarton. What can I do for you today?'

'I know it may seem like an odd question, but do you remember cleaning my shoes a while ago?' I said.

'Of course. D.I. Antrim gave me a nice tip.'

'I made a joke about bringing you all of my shoes to polish.'

'I remember,' he said, looking at my bag with some alarm. 'You haven't really brought them, have you?'

'Goodness, no. You told me Mr Boulting had asked you the same question. Did you also clean his shoes that day?'

'Yes, I did. They were covered in mud. Like yours. I think he must have been in the rose bed with Dermot after he got knocked out. I told D.I. Antrim all about it.'

'Oh, I see,' I said. 'Thank you. I would like to speak to Mr Boulting if that would be possible. Harry and I are thinking of organising a party here.'

'I'm sure he'd be able to see you. Come with me and I'll take you to his office.'

We followed him to the right, past the reception desk and the Christmas tree, and towards the toilet block joining the main hotel with the conservatory. Boulting's door hung open and he sat behind his desk in his swivel chair, his brow furrowed as he scrutinised his computer screen. He turned to look at us as we entered and a fleeting expression of annoyance drifted across his features. The porter had disappeared again, probably to avoid being blamed for bringing us to disturb Boulting's work.

'Can I help you?' he said, in a tone that suggested he'd rather squeeze lemon juice into his eyes.

'I hope so,' I said, pulling up a chair.

'We've got some questions you might like to answer,' said Harry.

'I doubt it,' said Boulting.

'We've been to Devon to speak to Ray Colthard, or should I call him by his real name, Brian Tipping?'

Boulting froze.

'What's that got to do with me?' he stammered.

'I rather hoped you'd tell us,' I said. 'He's been blackmailing you. Why didn't you go to the police?'

'I don't know what you're talking about. You need to leave now.'

He stood up and glowered at me, but sat down again when he noticed Harry's jaw clenching and his chest puffing out.

'I'm sure Safe Haven can help us with that. Lydia Sheldon will be ecstatic to receive proof that you scammed them by pretending to have subsidence,' said Harry.

'You can't prove that.'

'Actually, we can. Dermot Murray is prepared to swear to it, and any structural engineer can check the building to confirm the lack of damage. Also, Dermot has been talking to the police about the chisel he found in the flower bed. Your porter told us you had mud all over your shoes that day too. What were you doing in the flower bed? I bet the police will fancy searching your office for the chisel, or did you put it somewhere else? It's only a matter of time before the walls close in around you.'

Boulting blanched.

'Why are you here? What's it got to do with you anyway?'

'We're not interested in you and your pathetic schemes. We need to know what happened on the night of Sharon Walsh's murder, and you may have key information you aren't even aware of.'

'Well, I didn't kill her if that's what you're asking. What possible motive could I have?'

'Why don't we go back to the beginning,' said Harry.

'The beginning?' said Boulting.

'When did Colthard start to blackmail you?' I asked.

Boulting deflated a little.

'About two years ago. After he got fired from Safe Haven.'

'He seemed to think you tipped them off.'

'I did. He held a sword over our heads, threatening to cancel the insurance on Tarton Manor House, when he knew we couldn't get a new insurer due to the subsidence. I called his boss anonymously and told him about the subsidence scam. They got rid of him straight away.'

'And what happened after they fired him?' said Harry.

'He turned up here, hysterical with fury, and desperate for money. He threatened to go to the police with evidence we had swindled Lydia Sheldon out of her family estate.'

'So you paid him? Do the Tippings know?'

'They know we're being blackmailed. I told them I hadn't met the blackmailer. They were happy for me to pay to keep him quiet.'

'Why did you tell Colthard to come during the wedding?'

'I got sick of him blackmailing us. I planned to scare him into quitting.'

'The flower pot?' said Harry.

'You loosened it?' I asked.

'Not me. Fintan Hurley. He turned up looking for work before the wedding. Personally, I suspected him of casing the joint for a possible burglary. I paid him to loosen it after hours. I gave him a key to the storeroom on the balcony. He locked himself in during the day and let himself out at night when nobody was around.'

'Fintan knew the pot was loose?'

'Yeah, him and his sister. A nasty pair.'

'Theresa knew about the pot as well?' I said.

'She came with him to the hotel. I thought it was odd, but who knows what she wanted.'

'Did you plan to drop the pot on Colthard?' said Harry.

'I had planned to, but I chickened out. The pot weighed a ton. I was afraid he could be badly injured and I only wanted to scare him.'

'Were you waiting for him when I saw you in the passageway?'

'Yes, but too many people were passing through. I realised I might hurt the wrong person, so I went back to my office.'

'You didn't see what happened to Sharon?' I said.

'No, but I heard the bang as the pot fell on her and then hit the floor. I came out of my office to see what the fuss was and a woman ran by, almost knocking me over.'

'A woman? Are you sure?' said Harry.

'Yes, I could smell her perfume, but it was too dark to see her face. She was short, and wore a jumpsuit or bellbottoms of some sort. I couldn't see the colour.'

'Did you tell the police this?' I said.

'No. They didn't ask me and I worried they might connect me to the pot, so I didn't offer any information.'

'Why are you telling us now?'

'I'm afraid. What if someone connected Fintan and me to the death of Sharon and thinks we have information that could lead to them? Fintan died unexpectedly, according to the police, but what if someone got rid of him? I'm worried I might be next. I need you to find the killer before they find me.'

Chapter 34

Harry and I drove home in a state of extreme excitement, talking over each other and rehearsing complex theories about the murderer. Who was the woman who bumped into Tim Boulting in the dark passageway outside his office after the murder? Boulting's version of the story seemed to bring Fintan back into focus as a possible murderer. But did Fintan have time to get back to the conservatory and come running over to the passageway with Theresa? It seemed to me that neither of them had time to drop the flower pot on Sharon, and still respond to the scream I emitted when I realised Sharon had died.

I couldn't help feeling that the brooch might be the key to everything. Had somebody planted it on Fintan or had he stolen it from beside Sharon's body? I didn't even know what the brooch looked like. But I could fix that in an instant. I sent a text to Flo asking her if she would text me a photograph of the brooch. She rang me back almost instantly.

'Where are you now?'

'I'm in the car with Harry on my way back from Tarton Manor House.'

'I'm not going to ask what you were doing there. I'm not allowed to send you a photograph, but now the case is being wound up, I can give you the brooch if you'd like it. After all, Sharon intended for you to have it. Why don't you get Harry to drop you at the station, and I'll sneak you through to collect it in the flesh?

'That would be amazing. We can drive home together while Harry buys a takeaway at the Chinese.'

'Great plan. See you shortly. By the way, Carol is at the desk. Don't tell her about the brooch. I'll pretend I'm taking a sample from you to eliminate you from the forensics.'

As Harry drove off, I entered the police station to find Carol Burns at reception. A sneer appeared on her face when she recognised me. She appeared unsteady on her feet and blotches marked her cheeks. I wondered if she had been drinking again.

'Well, if it isn't miss hoity toity, I think I'm a detective, Bowe.'

'Were you expecting someone else?' I said. 'George perhaps?'

'As if you would know where he is. He dumped you for that hussy months ago. And now she's dead and he's free again.'

My blood boiled at her disrespect for Sharon. She probably still harboured expectations that George would pick her next.

'He may be at Helen's. They're hanging out together these days.'

'Helen? Who's she?'

'My sister. They've always got on like a house on fire. I guess it was inevitable they'd end up going out.'

She wobbled on her heels and almost tipped onto the desk in shock.

'He's going out with your sister? He can't be. His wife is hardly cold in her grave.'

The internal door opened and Flo beckoned me in. I gave Carol a little wave and followed Flo into the station.

'What was all that about?' said Flo.

'Nothing. I think she's been on the sauce again.'

'She'll be gone next week. Sally Right is back from holiday. I've never missed anyone so much.'

We passed through the office at speed, hoping to go unnoticed, and entered Flo's lair down the back stairs. The yard where the hearses pulled in had been excavated down a couple of metres so they could park at the back door of the forensics laboratory. I steeled myself before entering as I had vivid memories of fainting when I had entered during an autopsy. The smell of the laboratory still made me queasy, body or no body.

'You've gone pale,' said Flo. 'Come into my office. I've got geranium diffuser in there.'

She shut the door behind me and I took a couple of deep breaths, managing to quell the nausea.

'Sit down. I've got the brooch in here. You'll need to sign for it.'

She rustled around in the evidence box marked Sharon Walsh/Carter and produced a Ziploc bag which she placed on the desk in front of me.

'Here you go. Isn't it gorgeous?'

My vision swam as I picked up the bag and peered through the plastic. I caught my breath as it came into focus. A beautiful Haskell lizard pin. I gasped.

'Oh! Holy crap.'

'What's up? Isn't it what you expected?'

'I've seen this brooch before.'

'Maybe in Grace's shop?'

'No. Someone was wearing it.'

'Could it be a copy? They probably sold loads of them.'

'In America perhaps. They tend to be rarer here and one of a kind.'

'But who was wearing it?'

'Carol Burns. In this station. She had it on her jacket a few days after the murder of Sharon Walsh.,' I said, shaking my head in disbelief.

'Oh my goodness. Are you sure?'

'Positive.'

'So, either she killed Sharon and took the brooch from the body as a trophy, or she found it beside the body and stole it.'

'Why would Carol steal a brooch from someone lying fatally injured on the floor? That's not normal behaviour. I'm going with the trophy theory.'

'Neither is killing someone, but I have to agree,' said Flo.

'Why did she do it? And why would she wear the brooch so soon after the murder?'

'Everyone at the station knew she lusted after George. They used to joke about it behind her back. Could jealousy be the motive?'

'People have killed for less. Imagine wearing the brooch to the station.'

'What a cheek. She must have been confident no one would recognise it.'

'No one except Grace Wong. But I've no doubt this is the same brooch. It's too much of a coincidence.'

'But if it's the same brooch, she must have killed Fintan Hurley too.'

'Agreed. Who else could have planted it on the body? She must have killed him to frame him for Sharon's murder.

'And she was in the perfect place to know on whom to plant it. The reception desk is the hub of all knowledge at the station.'

'We need to find someone who can arrest her right now. Who's in the office?'

'I saw Joe Brennan at his desk when we walked by.'

'Come on. Let's go.'

'What about the brooch?'

'I don't think you're done with it yet. Have you still got the tissue paper they found down the side of the sofa? I reckon you need to test it for Carol Burn's DNA.'

'We already tested it. There was an unidentified sample on the paper. Carol Burns will be on file as she works here. I'll get someone to check her DNA against the unknown sample.'

Flo put the brooch back into the evidence box and locked it into the cupboard. We ran up the stairs to the office. Flo puffed and panted at the top, bright red in the face.

'I need to go to the gym,' she said.

'You'd like the Fat Fighters classes that Ghita runs. You should come along one day.'

'Maybe.'

Ahead of us, Joe Brennan slipped out of his cubicle, pulling on his coat.

'Ah, P.C. Brennan, we need to talk to you urgently,' said Flo.

'Can't it wait? I've got a date tonight.'

'It's urgent. You need to arrest Carol Burns on suspicion of the murder of Sharon Walsh.'

He frowned at us.

'Did I hear that right? Carol Burns? But I need the D.I. to confirm it.'

'You've got to arrest her now or at least keep her at the station under some pretext. Can you tell her D.I. Antrim needs to speak to her urgently. We'll contact Antrim immediately and get him to come in.'

'What about D.I. Carter? He's probably nearer.'

'Conflict of interests,' I said. 'It has to be D.I. Antrim.'

'Okay. I'll do it. Wait here in my office and I'll take her to an interview room.'

'Quickly, she mustn't get away.'

When P.C. Brennan returned shaking his head, I felt a chill run down my spine.

'She's gone,' he said. 'She's abandoned the desk and left through the front door.'

'Gone mid shift?' said Flo. 'But where?'

I sighed.

'I know where she's gone and it's my fault.'

Chapter 35

To my intense relief, I managed to raise George on his cell phone on first try. Normally, he made me ring him several times, just to prove how busy he was.

'Hi Tan. What's up?'

'I don't want you to panic, but Helen's in danger. I need you to go round to her house immediately. Break in if you have to. We're on our way with P.C. Brennan.'

I heard him swearing as he dropped his phone. I waited for him to pick it up.

'Did I hear you right? What the hell's going on?'

'Believe me. You need to go now. Carol Burns murdered Sharon and Fintan, and she's on her way to hurt Helen.'

'Carol Burns? Seriously? Okay, I'm on my way. You'd better have proof of this.'

'Trust me.'

He rang off. P.C. Brennan requisitioned a squad car and Flo and I piled into the back seat. He got straight onto his radio asking for back up from D.I. Antrim. We didn't wait for help to arrive. Joe Brennan had always struck me as the quiet bloke in the background, but he turned into an Avenger in a squad car. His jaw became squarer and his gaze steely. Even Flo seemed impressed, elbowing me in the ribs in the back seat.

'I won't put on the emergency lights. We don't want to alert Carol we're on to her. You must stay in the car when we get there,' he said. 'It may be dangerous.'

'That's my sister in the house with the murderer. I can't promise anything.'

'I should have known, but at least I gave you instructions, even if you don't follow them. Try not to get in the way at least.'

We rolled to a halt outside Helen's terraced house, parking right behind George's car which pulled in ahead of us. George jumped out of the car and I noticed his jaw jutting out in a peculiar way. He turned to look at us and I could see the determination written all over his face.

'Is she here?' I said.

'That's her car.'

'What are you going to do?'

'Will you call Helen on her cell phone?'

'Sure.'

To my surprise, Helen answered, speaking normally.

'Hi Tan. What's up?'

'Oh nothing. Just calling to see how you are. Flo's coming over for Chinese. Why don't you join us?'

'I can't right now. I've got a guest.'

'Can they come too?'

'I don't think that would be a good idea, she's a friend of George's. She, um…'

I heard a shriek and the phone went dead.

'What happened?' said George.

'They're in the house together. Can you break the door down?'

'I don't think so. It's solid hardwood.'

My cell phone rang. Harry.

'Hey! Did you get lost? Mouse and I are going to start without you.'

'There's been an unexpected hitch. I need your help.'

'What's going on?'

'Sharon's murderer is Carol Burns and she's in Helen's house. We think she may be intending to harm her.'

'Because of George?'

'Yes. The mad old bat has a crush on him.'

'Hey!' said George. 'She's got taste at least.'

I rolled my eyes at him.

'Anyway, we're outside trying to decide how to get in.'

'Mouse and I can take the back lane between the terraces and jump over the garden wall. Does Helen leave the back door open?'

'Usually. But what if Carol spots you?'

'Create a diversion. It won't take us five minutes to get there. I'll text you when we're at the back door.'

'Be careful. She's killed at least two people already.'

'I'll go to the front door and strike up a conversation. She might let me in,' said George.

The five minutes until Harry texted me seemed to last forever. Helen's house looked like it always did, with the tasteful shutters in the window and the neat sitting room. I tried not to feel agitated, but the reality of the situation set in. My sister had invited a killer into her house. A shadow passed by the window, but nobody stopped to gaze outside.

'Do you think she saw us?'

'If that was Helen, she's probably pretending she didn't.'

My cell pinged. It sounded like Big Ben in the quiet street. A message from Harry. 'We're outside the back door'. I nodded at George. He motioned at P.C. Brennan to move the squad car out of sight further down the street. Flo and I hid behind George's car, squatting on the pavement. Flo's face soon turned crimson with effort. George crossed the street and rang the doorbell. After a short delay, Helen answered. Her expression didn't give anything away, but she was deathly pale.

'Oh, hi George. What are you doing here?'

'I thought you might like some company.'

'Actually, I'm a little busy right now. Can you come back later?'

'I don't think I will.'

Suddenly, a hand holding a kitchen knife snaked around Helen's neck. It was all I could do not to scream. Carol Burn's disembodied voice chilled the air with its flat tone.

'You'd better come in then.'

'Why don't you put down the knife and we can all talk calmly about this,' said George.

'I don't think so,' said Carol, putting the knife to Helen's throat.

I almost fainted, but I couldn't stay hidden.

'Don't you dare touch my sister,' I shouted, jumping up.

My action distracted her for a split second. Long enough for a larger hand to grab Carol's and expel the knife it held onto the street. Helen pulled away from Carol and George enfolded her in his arms. A tender look appeared on his face as he stroked her hair and whispered calming words. Carol Burns disappeared with a squeal. Seconds later her legs stuck out of the front door like the Wicked Witch of the West as Harry tied her with strips of floral material. I hoped Helen didn't notice the demise of her favourite table cloth. She smiled at me over George's shoulder.

'Is there something you haven't told me?' said Flo.

'Possibly,' I said. 'We could fill you in over a Chinese takeaway.'

'I've a feeling it might take longer than that.'

A squad car came down the street with blue lights flashing and pulled onto the pavement. D.I. Antrim and two uniformed officers got out and ran to the door. Harry had trussed Carol Burns up like a Christmas ham and she almost fell as he passed her over to be read her rights. D.I. Antrim raised an eyebrow when he saw Helen in George's arms, but he didn't comment.

'I see you've been busy, Ms Bowe.'

I bit my lip to prevent a snort of laughter escaping.

'It seems so.'

'Why you don't just join the force and make it official I'll never know.'

'I'm a little long in the tooth for that.'

'I suppose so. We'd better take her down to the station and get a statement. You lot can go home. We'll speak to you later. Except you, George. You'd better hear this too.'

Harry and Mouse came across the road and gave Flo and me a hug. We all wandered back to the Grotty Hovel where Hades had raided the box of prawn fried rice and knocked most of it on to the floor. I swept it up and put it in his bowl, but he turned up his nose and stalked out through the cat flap.

'Honestly,' I said. 'There's no pleasing some people.'

Chapter 36

After Carol Burns had been charged with the murder of Sharon Walsh and of Fintan Hurley, she went to Bronzefield prison on remand. D.I. Antrim took our statements and entered the lizard brooch back into evidence. The unidentified DNA on the tissue paper used to wrap it turned out to be from Carol, and as George said in a rare moment of humour 'wrapped up the case against her'. Carol did not contest the charges. She gave a full statement of her actions and motives, her need for people to understand how she had been wronged, greater than her need to stay quiet.

With Carol Burns confined to Bronzefield, life began to go back to normal in Seacastle. George took over the reins in the police station, and D.I. Antrim returned to Brighton, frustrated in his attempt to replace him once more. While the cogs of the machine re-engaged, the humans involved continued to be shaken by the turn of events and the repercussions which were pinball like in their spread and effect.

Harry returned to Devon to hang out with his brother and mend their relationship. I encouraged this development although I missed Harry like a limb or an organ. They had begun to renovate the spare bedroom in the tumbledown cottage and I got nightly reports of their progress, or lack of it. The warmth and happiness in Harry's voice were balm for my heartache. And as Harry himself had pointed out, I had Helen.

Or at least I had had Helen for a short time, because now she and George were an item and, as with all new couples, they spent the vast majority of their time hanging out on the desert island of their love. They spent every possible minute in each other's company, leaving the rest of us to roll our eyes and feel just a tiny bit jealous of their luck in finding each other. I discovered that I did not mind in the least. Harry had proved to be an effective vaccination against my lingering Carter infection and I no longer had fantasies about returning to the beige villa or my former vaunted position as wife of the D.I.

I was not the only person feeling lonely. Mouse had been greatly affected by the ghost of his phantom sibling, more than he would admit. He had always been a big softy, but he cooed at babies in the street and lost all inclination to pretend to be macho any more. Luckily his friend Goose's wife had produced a cute baby girl, and was more than happy to let Mouse babysit and hang out with the baby, while she got some sleep. It did a lot to heal his shock at the deception and loss he felt for something which never existed. He would be a wonderful father someday but for now he enjoyed practicing with second hand babies.

Despite the unplanned ending to the Carter wedding, Rohan and Kieron had received many compliments on the delicious food at the reception. They had also fielded countless inquiries about their availability to cater other weddings and various functions from the small to the over the top enormous. Ghita had taken great heart from this, and her worries about Surfusion being a success had receded. She celebrated by producing yet another spectacular new cake flavour, which she brought to the Vintage for a tasting.

Roz blew in from a couple of days in the stormy seas with her husband Ed. He had taken to his bed with exhaustion, but she had an infinite battery. She cycled through the rain to the shop to try the new cake, closely followed by Grace who was dwarfed by her enormous raincoat. Flo could not come as she had a particularly tricky forensic puzzle to solve and had shut the door to her office and switched off her phone. We all understood that particular veto and respected her professionalism, leaving her to crack the code in peace.

Helen and Joy turned up too, windswept and laughing at their wild hairdos. Soon the café filled with laughter and the hiss of the Gaggia as we made our favourite coffees. Ghita, pink with excitement, whipped the linen dishcloth off the cake to reveal a lurid pink-iced cake with fresh raspberries clinging to the shiny surface.

'May I present a white chocolate and raspberry sponge cake with a hint of crème de framboise,' she said. 'It's a little bit naughty.'

'How many million calories a slice?' I said.

'I need a large piece. I've been hauling in nets for the past two nights,' said Roz.

'I didn't know they called it that over here,' said Grace, droll to the last.

'So, are you going to explain what happened to Sharon Walsh,' said Ghita. 'I don't understand any of this. I don't even know who Carol Burns is.'

'I think you met her a couple of times. She worked in the police station at the reception desk for many years. I remember her being there when I married George. She never liked me, but I didn't realise she had a serious crush on George. Her jealousy ate her up, and she drank more and more over the years. She wouldn't accept treatment and eventually they forced her to take early retirement.'

'Is that when Sharon took over from her?' said Joy.

'Yes. And when George decided to move on from our marriage. Carol had been ecstatic when George and I broke up, until she realised why. Her hatred of Sharon ate at her for months before she heard Sharon and George were getting married because Sharon had become pregnant.'

'Poor woman. Terrible taste. Who would have believed anyone could have fallen so hard for George.'

'Hang on there,' I said. 'He has his good points.'

'Obviously something that has universal appeal in your family,' said Roz, causing a chorus of jeering and laughing.

Helen blushed, and pretended to be cross, but could only produce a tolerant smile like a woman in love. I rolled my eyes at her and shook my head, producing another round of laughter from my friends.

'Whatever you do, don't get married in Tarton Manor House. It's got a history of bad luck,' said Mouse.

I punched his arm.

'Honestly, that's not funny.'

But it was.

'What happened on the night of the wedding?' said Ghita. 'Did Carol plan it all along?'

'Weirdly, Fintan Hurley loosened the flower pot after all, but not for himself. A man called Ray Colthard had been blackmailing Tim Boulting, the manager of the hotel, for years over an insurance scam. Boulting decided he could take it no longer and planned to scare Colthard off.'

'But what has Colthard got to do with the hotel?' said Joy.

'His real name is Brian Tipping. He's the nephew of the owners. It's a long story.'

'Go on, Tan. What happened next?' said Roz.

'Well, Tim Boulting gave up on his plan to drop the flower pot, when he saw how difficult it would be to target Colthard with all the people milling about. But meanwhile, Carol Burns had seen George having a massive row with Sharon and decided to intercede.'

'What was the row about?' said Ghita.

'Sharon confessed she had lost the baby. As a matter of fact, she had never been pregnant after all, but it doesn't matter now. Mouse sent George to the men's changing room to calm down, and Carol followed him up, but she lost her nerve and didn't go in. She saw Sharon waiting for me underneath her and noticed that the pot on the balcony had been loosened. She took it as a sign and she pushed the gargoyle off the balcony in a temper, intending to scare or injure her.'

'But it killed her instead. What a horrible outcome,' said Joy. 'Do we believe she genuinely made a mistake?'

'She swears she couldn't believe it when Sharon died. She rushed downstairs and quickly realised Sharon wouldn't recover. The brooch Sharon had bought for me had been dropped into the blood and Carol grabbed it. She realised she had seconds to get away, and she ran upstairs to hide in the women's changing room. She couldn't believe it when no one came up to check. They taped off the men's changing room and the balcony, but for some reason, it never occurred to them to search the other side. Carol snuck out later and she took the brooch home with her as a trophy.'

'But why did she kill Fintan?' said Ghita.

'Fintan had seen her go up to the balcony and threatened to expose her. He tried to blackmail her, but she wouldn't pay him. She realised Fintan was an easy mark after hearing the circumstantial evidence about him at the station. So she took the brooch and went to see him on the pretext of making a payment. He let her into his flat and she hit him when he turned his back on her. She framed him for Sharon's murder by planting the brooch on him. D.I. Antrim was desperate to close the case out and he took the easy way out. They were still looking for Fintan's murderer, but in all the wrong places.'

'What about Theresa?' said Joy. 'What happened to her?'

'I believe she returned to Liverpool to be with her family. There's nothing here for her now. She sold her company to a distributor.'

'Poor woman. She lost her sister and her husband in a matter of weeks,' said Ghita.

'But what about Colthard and Boulting?' said Roz. 'Boulting knocked out my cousin Dermot. He should get done for assault.'

'Helping the police with their inquiries. The Brighton boys have started a major fraud investigation into the goings on at Tarton Manor Hall. It seems likely the Tippings will go to jail, along with their nephew and Tim Boulting.'

'And Lydia Sheldon?' said Helen.

'Ah. That may be the only good thing to come out of this whole sorry tale.'

'Will she get the house back?' said Mouse.

'The Tippings swindled her out of it, so it seems the story may come full circle.'

'Now that's amazing,' said Roz. 'Dermot will be thrilled.'

'I'm still not getting married there,' said Helen. 'Who wants another coffee?'

Chapter 37

After the meet up at the Vintage, I took myself and a bag of scraps to sit in the wind shelter near the Grotty Hovel. The sun had recently set and the sky still had pink swirls of farewell in it. When Herbert did not approach after ten minutes, I stood and flung the contents of the bag into the wind. Soon a gathering of raucous herring gulls congregated to fight over the spoils. I watched them bickering and taking off with their trophies in their beaks.

I found myself thinking about the brooch Sharon had bought for me. There didn't seem to be any way I could enjoy wearing it with its history. Perhaps Grace would take it back and hide it among its brethren to be purchased by an unsuspecting collector and spirited into a drawer on someone's dresser. I might even persuade Grace to swap it for another. She had reminded me at the Vintage that I had agreed to help her with the fair at Shoreham, and asked me if I still wanted to do it. She's an odd stick, old Gracey, a combination of cool and fierce, with a filling of vulnerability. I intend to get to know her better.

Mouse came and found me at the shelter, his bonny face poking around the edge.

'I knew you'd be here,' he said. 'I brought us a flask of tea with a nip of whisky in it. Oh, and a warm blanket.'

We wrapped it around our knees and sipped our tea looking out at the fast-encroaching tide and the faster falling night. The lights of the wind farm twinkled in the distance interspersed with those of a fleet of large tankers heading for Rotterdam or Antwerp or some large European port. The occasional cry of a seabird heading home broke through the sound of the waves rinsing the pebbles like an eternal dish washer. Mouse sighed theatrically.

'What's up,' I asked, knowing I should.

'Life is very complicated,' he said. 'I think I won't grow up any more for a while. Do you mind if I stay at the Grotty Hovel until I feel braver?'

'You can stay forever if you want.'

'What if I get married?'

'You're not to get married before me, but you can still stay if she wants to.'

'And when are you getting married?'

'Soon.'

'How soon?'

'I don't know. Haven't you had enough of weddings for the time being?'

'Now that you mention it.'

Other books

The Seacastle Mysteries - a cosy mystery series set on the south coast of England

Deadly Return (Book 1)

Staying away is hard, but returning may prove fatal. Tanya Bowe, a former investigative journalist, is adjusting to life as an impoverished divorcee in the seaside town of Seacastle. She crosses paths with a long-lost schoolmate, Melanie Conrad, during a house clearance to find stock for her vintage shop. The two women renew their friendship, but their reunion takes a tragic turn when Mel is found lifeless at the foot of the stairs in the same house.

While the police are quick to label Mel's death as an accident, Tanya's gut tells her there's more to the story. Driven by her instincts, she embarks on her own investigation, delving into Mel's mysterious past. As she probes deep into the Conrad family's secrets, Tanya uncovers a complex web of lies and blackmail. But the further she digs, the more intricate the puzzle becomes. As Tanya's determination grows, so does the shadow of danger. Each new revelation brings her closer to a chilling truth. Can she unravel the secrets surrounding Mel's demise before the killer strikes again?

Eternal Forest (Book 2)

What if proving a friend's husband innocent of murder implicates her instead?

Tanya Bowe, an ex-investigative journalist, and divorcee, runs a vintage shop in the coastal town of Seacastle. When her old friend, Lexi Burlington-Smythe borrows the office above the shop as a base for the campaign to create a kelp sanctuary off the coast, Tanya is thrilled with the chance to get involved and make some extra money. Tanya soon gets drawn into the high-stake arguments surrounding the campaign, as tempers are frayed, and her friends, Roz and Ghita favour opposing camps. When a celebrity eco warrior is murdered, the evidence implicates Roz's husband Ed, and Tanya finds her loyalties stretched to breaking point as she struggles to discover the true identity of the murderer.

Fatal Tribute (Book 3)

How do you find the murderer, when every act is convincing? Tanya Bowe, an ex-investigative journalist, agrees to interview the contestants of the National Talent Competition for the local newspaper, but finds herself up to her neck in secrets, sabotage and simmering resentment. The tensions increase when her condescending sister comes to stay next door for the duration of the contest.

Several rising stars on the circuit hope to win the competition, but old stager, Lance Emerald, is not going down without a fight. When Lance is found dead in his dressing room, Tanya is determined to find the murderer but complex dynamics between the contestants and fraught family relationships make the mystery harder to solve. Can Tanya uncover the truth before another murder takes centre stage?

Mortal Vintage (Book 5)
Up for pre-order shortly

Other books by the Author
I write under various pen names in different genres. If you are looking for another mystery, why don't you try **Mortal Mission,** written as Pip Skinner.

Mortal Mission
Will they find life on Mars, or death?
When the science officer for the first crewed mission to Mars dies suddenly, backup Hattie Fredericks gets the coveted place on the crew. But her presence on the Starship provokes suspicion when it coincides with a series of incidents which threaten to derail the mission.

After a near-miss while landing on the planet, the world watches as Hattie and her fellow astronauts struggle to survive. But, worse than the harsh elements on Mars, is their growing realisation that someone, somewhere, is trying to destroy the mission.

When more astronauts die, Hattie doesn't know who to trust. And her only allies are 35 million miles away. As the tension ratchets up, violence and suspicion invade both worlds. If you like science-based sci-fi and a locked-room mystery with a twist, you'll love this book.

The Green Family Saga

Rebel Green – Book 1

Relationships fracture when two families find themselves caught up in the Irish Troubles.

The Green family move to Kilkenny from England in 1969, at the beginning of the conflict in Northern Ireland. They rent a farmhouse on the outskirts of town, and make friends with the O'Connor family next door. Not every member of the family adapts easily to their new life, and their differing approaches lead to misunderstandings and friction. Despite this, the bonds between the family members deepen with time.

Perturbed by the worsening violence in the North threatening to invade their lives, the children make a pact never to let the troubles come between them. But promises can be broken, with tragic consequences for everyone.

Africa Green – Book 2

Will a white chimp save its rescuers or get them killed?

Journalist Isabella Green travels to Sierra Leone, a country emerging from civil war, to write an article about a chimp sanctuary. Animals that need saving are her obsession, and she can't resist getting involved with the project, which is on the verge of bankruptcy. She forms a bond with local boy, Ten, and army veteran, Pete, to try and save it. When they rescue a rare white chimp from a village frequented by a dangerous rebel splinter group, the resulting media interest could save the sanctuary. But the rebel group have not signed the cease fire. They believe the voodoo power of the white chimp protects them from bullets, and they are determined to take it back so they can storm the capital. When Pete and Ten go missing, only Isabella stands in the rebels' way. Her love for the chimps unlocks the fighting spirit within her. Can she save the sanctuary or will she die trying?

Fighting Green – Book 3

Liz Green is desperate for a change. The Dot-Com boom is raging in the City of London, and she feels exhausted and out of her depth. Added to that, her long-term boyfriend, Sean O'Connor, is drinking too much and shows signs of going off the rails. Determined to start anew, Liz abandons both Sean and her job, and buys a near-derelict house in Ireland to renovate.

She moves to Thomastown where she renews old ties and makes new ones, including two lawyers who become rivals for her affection. When Sean's attempt to win her back goes disastrously wrong, Liz finishes with him for good. Finding herself almost penniless, and forced to seek new ways to survive, Liz is torn between making a fresh start and going back to her old loves.
Can Liz make a go of her new life, or will her past become her future?

The Sam Harris Series (written as PJ Skinner)

Set in the late 1980's and through the 1990's, the thrilling Sam Harris Adventure series navigates through the career of a female geologist. Themes such as women working in formerly male domains, and what constitutes a normal existence, are developed in the context of Sam's constant ability to find herself in the middle of an adventure or mystery. Sam's home life provides a contrast to her adventures and feeds her need to escape. Her attachment to an unfaithful boyfriend is the thread running through her romantic life, and her attempts to break free of it provide another side to her character.

The first book in the Sam Harris Series sets the scene for the career of an unwilling heroine, whose bravery and resourcefulness are needed to navigate a series of adventures set in remote sites in Africa and South America. Based loosely on the real-life adventures of the author, the settings and characters are given an authenticity that will connect with readers who enjoy adventure fiction and mysteries set in remote settings with realistic scenarios.

Fool's Gold - Book 1

Newly qualified geologist Sam Harris is a woman in a man's world - overlooked, underpaid but resilient and passionate. Desperate for her first job, and nursing a broken heart, she accepts an offer from notorious entrepreneur Mike Morton, to search for gold deposits in the remote rainforests of Sierramar. With the help of nutty local heiress, Gloria Sanchez, she soon settles into life in Calderon, the capital. But when she accidentally uncovers a long-lost clue to a treasure buried deep within the jungle, her journey really begins. Teaming up with geologist Wilson Ortega, historian Alfredo Vargas and the mysterious Don Moises, they venture through the jungle, where she lurches between excitement and insecurity. Yet there is a far graver threat looming; Mike and Gloria discover that one of the members of the expedition is plotting to seize the fortune for himself and is willing to do anything to get it. Can Sam survive and find the treasure or will her first adventure be her last?

Hitler's Finger - Book 2

The second book in the Sam Harris Series sees the return of our heroine Sam Harris to Sierramar to help her friend Gloria track down her boyfriend, the historian, Alfredo Vargas. Geologist Sam Harris loves getting her hands dirty. So, when she learns that her friend Alfredo has gone missing in Sierramar, she gives her personal life some much needed space and hops on the next plane. But she never expected to be following the trail of a devious Nazi plot nearly 50 years after World War II ... Deep in a remote mountain settlement, Sam must uncover the village's dark history. If she fails to reach her friend in time, the Nazi survivors will ensure Alfredo's permanent silence. Can Sam blow the lid on the conspiracy before the Third Reich makes a devastating return?

The background to the book is the presence of Nazi war criminals in South America which was often ignored by locals who had fascist sympathies during World War II. Themes such as tacit acceptance of fascism, and local collaboration with fugitives from justice are examined and developed in the context of Sam's constant ability to find herself in the middle of an adventure or mystery.

The Star of Simbako - Book 3

A fabled diamond, a jealous voodoo priestess, disturbing cultural practices. What could possibly go wrong? The third book in the Sam Harris Series sees Sam Harris on her first contract to West Africa to Simbako, a land of tribal kingdoms and voodoo. Nursing a broken heart, Sam Harris goes to Simbako to work in the diamond fields of Fona. She is soon involved with a cast of characters who are starring in their own soap opera, a dangerous mix of superstition, cultural practices, and ignorance (mostly her own). Add a love triangle and a jealous woman who wants her dead and Sam is in trouble again. Where is the Star of Simbako? Is Sam going to survive the chaos?

This book is based on visits made to the Paramount Chiefdoms of West Africa. Despite being nominally Christian communities, Voodoo practices are still part of daily life out there. This often leads to conflicts of interest. Combine this with the horrific ritual of FGM and it makes for a potent cocktail of conflicting loyalties. Sam is pulled into this life by her friend, Adanna, and soon finds herself involved in goings on that she doesn't understand.

The Pink Elephants - Book 4

Sam gets a call in the middle of the night that takes her to the Masaibu project in Lumbono, Africa. The project is collapsing under the weight of corruption and chicanery engendered by management, both in country and back on the main company board. Sam has to navigate murky waters to get it back on course, not helped by interference from people who want her to fail. When poachers invade the elephant sanctuary next door, her problems multiply. Can Sam protect the elephants and save the project or will she have to choose?

The fourth book in the Sam Harris Series presents Sam with her sternest test yet as she goes to Africa to fix a failing project. The day-to-day problems encountered by Sam in her work are typical of any project manager in the Congo which has been rent apart by warring factions, leaving the local population frightened and rootless. Elephants with pink tusks do exist, but not in the area where the project is based. They are being slaughtered by poachers in Gabon for the Chinese market and will soon be extinct, so I have put the guns in the hands of those responsible for the massacre of these defenceless animals.

The Bonita Protocol - Book 5

An erratic boss. Suspicious results. Stock market shenanigans. Can Sam Harris expose the scam before they silence her? It's 1996. Geologist Sam Harris has been around the block, but she's prone to nostalgia, so she snatches the chance to work in Sierramar, her old stomping ground. But she never expected to be working for a company that is breaking all the rules. When the analysis results from drill samples are suspiciously high, Sam makes a decision that puts her life in peril. Can she blow the lid on the conspiracy before they shut her up for good? The Bonita Protocol sees Sam return to Sierramar and take a job with a junior exploration company in the heady days before the Bre-X crash. I had fun writing my first megalomaniac female boss for this one. I have worked in a few junior companies with dodgy bosses in the past, and my only comment on the sector is buyer beware…

Digging Deeper - Book 6
A feisty geologist working in the diamond fields of West Africa is kidnapped by rebels. Can she survive the ordeal or will this adventure be her last? It's 1998. Geologist Sam Harris is desperate for money so she takes a job in a tinpot mining company working in war-torn Tamazia. But she never expected to be kidnapped by blood thirsty rebels.

Working in Gemsite was never going to be easy with its culture of misogyny and corruption. Her boss, the notorious Adrian Black is engaged in a game of cat and mouse with the government over taxation. Just when Sam makes a breakthrough, the camp is overrun by rebels and Sam is taken captive. Will anyone bother to rescue her, and will she still be alive if they do?

I worked in Tamazia (pseudonym for a real place) for almost a year in different capacities. The first six months I spent in the field are the basis for this book. I don't recommend working in the field in a country at civil war but, as for many of these crazy jobs, I needed the money.

Concrete Jungle - Book 7 (series end)
Armed with an MBA, Sam Harris is storming the City - But has she swapped one jungle for another?

Forging a new career was never going to be easy, and Sam discovers she has not escaped from the culture of misogyny and corruption that blighted her field career.

When her past is revealed, she finally achieves the acceptance she has always craved, but being one of the boys is not the panacea she expected. The death of a new friend presents her with the stark choice of compromising her principals to keep her new position, or exposing the truth behind the façade. Will she finally get what she wants or was it all a mirage?

I did an MBA to improve my career prospects, and much like Sam, found it didn't help much. In the end, it's only your inner belief that counts. What other people say, or think, is their problem. I hope you enjoy this series. I wrote it to rid myself of demons, and it worked.

Box Sets

Sam Harris Adventure Box Set Book 2-4
Sam Harris Adventure Box Set Book 5-7
Sam Harris Adventure Box Set Books 2-7

Connect with the Author

About the Author

I write under several pen names and in various genres: PJ Skinner (Travel Adventures and Cozy/Cosy Mystery), Pip Skinner (Sci-Fi), Kate Foley (Irish contemporary), and Jessica Parkin (children's illustrated books).

I moved to the south coast of England just before the Covid pandemic and after finishing my trilogy, The Green Family Saga, I planned the Seacastle Mysteries. I have always been a massive fan of crime and mystery and I guess it was inevitable I would turn my hand to a mystery series eventually.

Before I wrote novels, I spent 30 years working as an exploration geologist, managing remote sites and doing due diligence of projects in over thirty countries. During this time, I collected the tall tales and real-life experiences which inspired the Sam Harris Adventure Series, chronicling the adventures of a female geologist as a pioneer in a hitherto exclusively male world.

I worked in many countries in South America and Africa in remote, strange, and often dangerous places, and loved every minute, despite encountering my fair share of misogyny and other perils. The Sam Harris Adventure Series is for lovers of intelligent adventure thrillers happening just before the time of mobile phones and the internet. It has a unique viewpoint provided by Sam, a female interloper in a male world, as she struggles with alien cultures and failed relationships.

My childhood in Ireland inspired me to write the Green Family Saga, which follows the fortunes of an

English family who move to Ireland just before the start of the troubles.

I have also written a mystery on Mars, inspired by my fascination with all things celestial. It is a science-based murder mystery, think The Martian with fewer potatoes and more bodies.

~~~~~~~~~~~~~~~~~~~~~~~~~~~~~~~~

Follow me on Amazon to get informed of my new releases. Just put PJ Skinner into the search box on Amazon and then click on the follow button on my author page.

Please subscribe to my Seacastle Mysteries <u>Newsletter</u> for updates and offers by using this QR code

You can also use the QR code below to get to my website for updates and to buy paperbacks direct from me.

You can also follow me on <u>Twitter</u>, Instagram, Tiktok, or on <u>Facebook</u> @pjskinnerauthor